ORDERS!

"En route to rendezvous you're to give Petreac a wide berth. The Hukk have been secretly assembling squadrons of raiders there for months now. And you're to take up station here on the left of the fleet point. Officially, this is a propaganda maneuver. However—if by some miscalculation the Softliners happen to be wrong and the Hukk do jump you—prematurely . . . which they might well do if you appear to be making a feint in their direction . . . and if you should just happen to blast a few squadrons of Hukk raiders out of space *before* Starbird has time to order you to turn the other cheek, . . ." Kelvin stopped and looked balefully at Dalton.

"Sounds like fun!" said Dalton.

Books by Keith Laumer

The Best of Keith Laumer
Fat Chance
The Glory Game
A Plague of Demons
Retief and the Warlords
Retief: Emissary to the Stars
Retief of the CDT
Retief's War

Published by POCKET BOOKS

THE GLORY GAME

Keith Laumer

PUBLISHED BY POCKET BOOKS NEW YORK

POCKET BOOKS, a Simon & Schuster division of
GULF & WESTERN CORPORATION
1230 Avenue of the Americas, New York, N.Y. 10020

ISBN: 0-671-83060-0

First Pocket Books printing March, 1980

10 9 8 7 6 5 4 3 2 1

Trademarks registered in the United States and other countries.

Printed in the U.S.A.

THE GLORY GAME

CHAPTER ONE

It was after one o'clock when Commodore Tancredi Dalton left his room. The lobby of the Ranking Officers' Billet was crowded with military and civilian personnel: officers in uniform and mufti, high-level officials of the Department, newsmen, diplomats, a few wives and some less formal female companions. The air, Dalton thought, was somewhat like that of a cruise ship just before departure rather than of a military headquarters on the eve of action—although the impending "action" was, of course, to be merely fleet maneuvers in force, showing the flag in the vicinity of Piranha, to let the Hukk know that their activities in the area had not gone unnoticed.

CPO Bagarin, the Desk Officer, plump and obsequious, handed him a note as he signed out. It was written in an elegant feminine hand on faintly scented lilac paper:

If you're not here by twelve thirty—then I suppose I'll have to wait. Hurry, darling.

Arianne

"May I call a car for you, Commodore?" Bagarin inquired, reaching for a button.

"No thanks," Dalton said. "I need the exercise."

"Conditions in town today are a bit, ah, unruly, Commodore," Bagarin said; his small eyes almost disappeared in the folds around them, though he was not a really fat man. His hand hovered over the button. "I'd better get a car round for you after all."

"That's thoughtful of you, Chief," Dalton said. "But it won't be necessary." He turned away.

"But, sir—I've . . ." Bagarin's petulant voice was lost in the hubbub of conversation as Dalton crossed to the twenty-foot-wide glass entry. He stepped through into the cool, slightly pepper-and-sawdust-smelling air of the world known as Aldo Cerise. The Deck Police guards on duty came to attention as he went down the broad steps. A large black groundcar with a CDT crest and a cased rank flag was parked in the street a few yards distant; Dalton saw the driver straighten, reach for the ignition switch. He continued on his way without pausing.

He heard the car's turbines whirl up to speed. On impulse, he stepped into the shelter of a deep doorway and paused, miming the lighting of a cigarette. The big car rolled past, the driver scanning the crowd with an anxious expression. Dalton waited until the car turned left into Concordiat Way before emerging.

It was a bright, cool day. Aldo's big, gentle, amber sun hung almost at zenith, shedding a soft technicolor light over the narrow street. The shops, manned by descendants of the settlers of two hundred years earlier, were open and doing a thriving business among the off-duty Naval personnel, hawking souvenirs, garish local handicrafts, quaint gift items, foods and shore clothes. The Terrans were conspicuous among the Aldans. The latter, while completely human, had evolved a distinct somatype: short-statured, dark-haired, with skin of an almost greenish tan. They had large mouths which seemed always to be open, displaying fine sets of large, square, brownish teeth. Some of the more enterprising of them plucked at Dalton's arm as he passed, walking briskly up the slightly sloping street.

His route quickly took him out of the overcrowded quarter surrounding the ROB. He climbed a flight of wide, steep stone steps cut into what had once been a cliff under which the first settlers had established their town, emerged on a wide quiet avenue shaded by imported Terran linden trees. In their amber shade, he strolled past the demure facades of elegant shops and exclusive restaurants which catered to the diplomatic set whose grand residences occupied the crest above, glimpsed occasionally through the trees clothing the slope.

The Terran Embassy was a haughty glass front rising featureless among the more graceful structures that flanked it. A short black-surfaced drive swung in between stainless steel pillars, sweeping past the high, blank slab of the polished heowood door. On the portico, a Marine, gorgeous in the traditional blues, stood at rigid parade rest, white-gloved left hand behind him, right hand gripping the chrome-plated, ebony-stocked power rifle grounded beside his polished right toe. He snapped to and executed a rifle salute with the precision of a machine. Dalton nodded and went in.

There was no crowd here; a sleek young woman

with a hushed voice directed Dalton to the lounge. In the dimness of the long, low room rank badges and jewels glittered; soft music provided an unobtrusive background to a murmur of well-bred conversation. The cool air smelled of mint and tobacco and expensive brandy.

Arianne was at a table at the far side of the room, surrounded by a group of well-fed men of middle age and beyond. Dalton recognized Arianne's father, Senator Kelvin, large and bland; Rear Admiral Coign, small and spare; Vice Admiral Hayle, square and bluff; and a number of lesser Naval lights. There was also a pinch-faced civilian with shiny black hair who looked up sharply as Dalton came up. Kelvin greeted Dalton by name.

"So you didn't really stand me up after all, darling," Arianne said in her breathy contralto. She was a slender brunette with wide eyes and a soft mouth. In her colorful gauzy frock she looked very young and high-bred, like a fresh-blossomed prize crocus among cacti, Dalton thought.

"Let up on him, girl, he's a busy man," Kelvin said in the hearty manner he always employed among inferiors. His sharp black eyes were on Dalton's. "I'm sure you gentlemen know the commodore by sight as well as by reputation," he said to the others. He introduced the civilian as Assistant Undersecretary of Defense Lair.

"I take it you feel everything's under control in your command, Dalton," the rear admiral said shortly. His tone indicated he doubted it.

"I assure you I wouldn't be here if it weren't, sir," Dalton said almost offhandedly as he took a seat beside the girl. She gave him a look which he thought was probably intended to be meaningful. And it wasn't hard to guess the meaning:

Now, behave yourself—at least as long as Father's beady eye is on you. . . .

In return he gave her a deliberately ambiguous smile, and said, "Sorry to be late; last-minute details, you know."

"Why do they always have to come up at the last minute, Tan?"

"They wouldn't be last-minute details if they didn't. By the way, Senator—did you send a car over to the billet for me, sir?"

"Why, no, I assumed—"

"I wasn't complaining, Senator; just curious."

"You're commanding a flotilla, aren't you, Commodore?" a youngish captain spoke up. "You don't happen to have a slot open for a fire-eating gunnery officer, do you?"

"Ask the admiral," Dalton said. "I just work here."

"I'm still not at all sure," Coign said testily, "just why it is that a flotilla was given to a man of your rank, Dalton." He glanced at the civilian. "Don't we have enough senior flag officers available to command our fleets, Mr. Undersecretary?"

"As to that"—the civilian started hesitantly—

"They gave Dalton his command because they're smart enough back in the Department to know a good combat officer when they see one," Admiral Hayle spoke up. "They don't like him much, you understand, Fred; he makes too many waves; that's why he didn't get the stars to go with the job." He winked at Arianne and finished his brandy at a gulp.

"The admiral's just having his little joke, Mr. Lair," the senator put in heartily. "He understands that the problems of the Joint Chiefs—"

"Never mind, Senator," Hayle said genially, "I'm

too old to fire, and I've got too many medals. They'd have to take 'em all back first, and that would be embarrassing all around, eh, Mr. Lair?"

"I don't pretend to have the grasp of military matters that you professional officers do," Lair snapped with surprising heat, "but I can assure you that department policy—whether it regards personnel or administration or operations—is not arrived at impulsively."

"On that note," Arianne said, "Tan and I will take our departure. Come on, Tan; I was ready for lunch half an hour ago."

"You'll find the prime ribs exceptional," the senator said, rising as Arianne and Dalton got to their feet.

"I don't want to eat in the stuffy old embassy dining room again, Tan," the girl said. "Let's go into the city somewhere. I want to see some of the real Aldo while I'm here."

"I wouldn't recommend that," the senator said heavily. "The town's swarming with sailors, and the kind who prey off them. No place for a young woman."

"Tan will be with me," Arianne said, almost reprimandingly. "I feel perfectly safe under his protection —even if he *is* a sailor."

"Oh, for heaven's sake, I didn't mean—"

"I know what you mean, Senator," Coign said sharply, "and I agree completely. Some of the men we've had to accept aboard our ships—draftees, reservists . . ."

"That's the trouble with a war, isn't it, Admiral?" Arianne said sweetly. "You have to have men to fight it." The emphasis on "men" was slight but unmistakable.

"Now who's baiting tigers?" Dalton asked as they made their way among the tables.

"Those old fuddies ought to be retired to a home for elderly spinsters," she said, then laughed. "The look on Goldy Coign's face was a prize; too bad I couldn't frame it to hang over the mantel."

2

They paused in the foyer long enough for Dalton to make a call, then summoned down one of the spinners that hovered nearby, on call. Below them, the city was a sprawl of toy blocks spilled down the mountainside to the sea. The port was visible twenty miles away as a vast sugar-white rectangle, where here and there an intolerably brilliant spark glittered and winked.

"I suppose the fleet's all ready to go," Arianne said without enthusiasm. "What a terrible waste—all those men, all that superb equipment—sent out to risk being battered and smashed in a senseless war."

"We have to face the Hukk now," Dalton said, "or later, at a less favorable time."

Arianne eyed him obliquely. "I never thought I'd hear you spouting the Hardline."

"Not exactly the Hardline," Dalton said, smiling. "The Dalton line."

"It's not the Navy line, either."

"Agreed."

"Tan, you're going to destroy yourself yet with your stubborn insistence on having your own way. You're a career man, not a . . . a Belt prospector! You have all the advantages of your position; why can't you accept the limitations of it?"

"Maybe I have a different view of the advantages, so-called, and the limitations too," Dalton said, not quite so genially.

"I'm sure you do, Tan," Arianne said quickly. "I didn't mean to imply irresponsibility. You're the most responsible man I know. That's just the point—you're *not* responsible for Navy policy. Your function is to carry out orders." She shook her head. "And I didn't mean that the way it sounded, either, Tan. Navy policy isn't evolved in a vacuum. Lots of good men—including the Council—have studied these things, probably far more exhaustively than you've had any opportunity to do—and they've evolved a course of action. It's up to you to use your abilities—and the office they've entrusted to you—to carry out their policies. Anything else is—anarchy."

"It's not quite that simple," Dalton said. "We like to simplify things, to try to scale complex matters down to a level we can understand. It's helpful sometimes. I suppose if we weren't able to do it, we'd never accomplish anything. But all the while we should remember: It's simplification."

The spinner deposited them on the roof of the Terran Club. They descended into the air-conditioned, scented, sound-proofed dining room and took a table on the glassed-in terrace overlooking the marketplace. The dinner was superb: Terran pheasant, mutant artichokes from Flamme, local greens and native kimnuts—one of the few indigenous products assimilable by the Terran metabolism.

"It was lovely, Tan," Arianne said after coffee and brandy. "But it wasn't really Aldo. I want to actually *see* the city; feel it, smell it, touch it."

"It's essentially a Terran town," Dalton said. "The first settlers picked an uninhabited spot to plant their colony. It's no more alien than a town in Morocco, say, or Laos. Maybe less."

"What are the real native towns like?"

"They're not what we'd call towns, really. Prairie

dog villages, maybe; tunnels, burrows, grouped around water holes. They're not very intelligent, you know; smarter than a porpoise or a chimp but low-grade moron by human standards."

"We shouldn't apply human standards to them," Arianne said with feeling. "They're *not* human—that's what makes them so unique, so . . . valuable."

"Emotionally, I agree with you. From a practical standpoint, we have to face the fact that they can only function at a certain level in the context of our technology—"

"Why should they have to function in the context of our technology? Why can't we just . . . leave them alone? Let them develop in their own way?"

"The human race has reached a point where it has to expand into space. Planet-bound, we'll choke in our own waste products, if not in this century, then in the next—or the one after. We have to live, and living means growth, and that implies expansion. A single planet can't hold us, Arianne. We have to go out, or die."

"Then maybe we want to die."

"You don't mean that," Dalton said casually.

Arianne opened her mouth as if to retort, but hesitated, then shook her head.

"No—of course I don't. But why are we here on Aldo? Why couldn't we limit ourselves to totally uninhabited worlds? Why does our advantage have to mean some other race's disadvantage?"

"You know as well as I do that worlds where we can live without artificial environment are rare, and every such world has evolved its own life—is the product of life."

"Of course. I just wish somehow it were different."

"So do I—in a way. And in another way, I accept the laws of nature. The fox is a beautiful animal. Without rabbits to live on, it would soon die out. That's nature. Who are we to decide unilaterally that the order of nature is wrong?"

"So we just go on, perpetuating a dog-eat-dog—or a fox-eat-bunny—existence?"

"No—but we have to remember to make the distinction between what's true and what we wish were true."

Arianne shook her head dismissingly. "That's enough deep conversation, Tan. I understand you—I think. I just hope the Navy brass does. Now—let's go somewhere and have fun."

Dalton signaled to a waiter, a "native" Aldan, who hurried over, showing his teeth in a smile. "I take it that by fun, you mean something unwise?" Dalton said after he had signed the chit.

"Naturally. Who wants to be wise all the time?"

"The old primate trait: climbing down out of a nice safe tree to see what it's like out on the grassland among the lions."

"Don't talk about me as if I were an anthropological specimen," Arianne said.

"But you are, my dear," Dalton said. "And so am I. That's what we have to keep in mind every time we're tempted to play God."

They left the club, took a native put-shaw down to the Old Town, a cluttered, cramped, colorful conglomerate of two-century-old prefabs and later-era stone and wood buildings. The crooked streets, lined with narrow shops redolent of Aldan cookery and inadequate drainage, were barely wide enough for two of the local power carts to pass, with much cursing of drivers. Arianne insisted on shopping the stalls on foot, gaily buying up local silks, carved bunstones and green wickerwork. The sun sank low in the sky; the thick, early dusk fell, submerging the street in umber shadows. Quite suddenly, the noise and the heat were gone; the shops put up their shutters; a cool breeze swept grit along the purplish cobbles.

"I'm tired," Arianne said. "And hungry." She clung to Dalton's arm, and he felt her shiver. "Suddenly it seems so alien, so far from home. How could they ever have done it—the first settlers? To come out here, so far away—with the primitive technology of two hundred years ago—to leave it all behind and try to start over in a strange world—and not even this sad little town, then, to give them shelter."

"They were brave, and tough—and desperate."

"And now it's all threatened by the Hukk. For the first time I'm beginning to see what the Hardline's all about, Tan."

"They did what they had to do. Now the Hukk are doing what *they* have to do. Our blunder was in not stopping them sooner—in using people like these as pawns."

"I don't understand you, Tan," Arianne said, pulling away from him. She looked searchingly into his face. "Just when I think I do—I don't."

"Never mind; let's do something about your appetite. Back to the Embassy—?"

"No . . . there." She pointed to a gaudy illuminated sign hanging crookedly over the street, illustrating a man—obviously an Aldan—at cards with a horned and hoofed devil done in glowing red.

"The Pot's Right is the most notorious dive in Old Town," Dalton said. "I might have known you'd find it."

"Don't patronize me, Tan; you brought me here." She tugged at his hand. "Let's go."

3

The patron met them at the door, bowing in the curious lopsided Aldan way, ushering them through a beaded hanging into the noise and body warmth and spice odors of a room packed with humanity. The crowd here differed vastly from those at the ROB and the Embassy; enlisted Naval personnel, civilian labor contractees, a few tourists out for thrills, a scattering of Aldan settlers aping Terran ways. Tables—too many for the available space—crowded close around the undersized dance floor where couples jittered and bounced out of time with the orchestra, which played with visible but inaudible energy, drowned out in the din of voices, the clash of crockery, the scrape of feet.

Dalton passed a bill to the maître d'hôtel, who palmed it and led the way through the press to a surprisingly good table under a balcony, close to the dance floor. He bestowed large green-and-gilt menus with the motif of the card players, bowed, and was swallowed up by the press.

"It's almost frightening," Arianne said, leaning across to speak to Dalton—a move which emphasized the nice contour of her breasts, modestly covered in the demure dress she wore. "If I'd known—"

"You'd have been twice as eager to come. The food's good, though. And the drinks are honest."

Conversation was impossible. Dalton ordered, and the service was quick. The food was plentiful, delicately seasoned, flavorful: a potpourri of rice, vegetables, and the snow-white meat of a native marine creature. They ate and watched the crowd. The sailors were boisterous but good-humored; the local bouncers were swift and efficient. Dalton and Arianne finished eating, and he ordered a local liqueur.

A spotlight dazzled down from above; a PA-amplified voice announced the floor show. The head-waiter appeared, bustling along with a party of six in his wake: three large, well-dressed men with gray hair, enough alike to be brothers, and three women, one lean, two plump, all extravagantly gowned and jeweled. A table was produced and set up at the edge of the floor, decked in a twinkling with linen, china, silver, glasses. The newcomers were seated, with flourishes, completely blocking the view of the floor from an adjacent table occupied by four sailors and their dates.

"That was a dirty trick," Arianne said, "putting those VIPs right in front of the boys."

A blocky Naval rating at the occluded table pushed back his chair, caught the headwaiter's sleeve as he passed.

"I paid you for a ringside table, Jack," he said. "All we can see is backs."

"Get your hands off me, sailor, unless you want me to have you and your whole party chucked out in the street," the headwaiter snarled.

The six new arrivals pointedly gazed in the opposite direction, ignoring the byplay.

"It's not that easy, Jack," the stocky man said tightly. "I've got plenty of friends here—"

The headwaiter had made an unobtrusive highsign; suddenly there were half a dozen large waiters encircling the sailor. Dalton saw the glint of metal in the hand of one who was easing up beside the headwaiter. He rose quickly and caught the headwaiter's wrist.

"Just a minute," Dalton said in a voice that cut through the chatter. "You wouldn't have been about to physically assault a member of the armed forces, would you, fellow?" He shook the man's wrist; a small spraysule dropped to the floor and was instantly kicked away by another waiter.

"Tan," Arianne said sharply, and subsided.

"What business—" the headwaiter started, rounding. He checked as he saw Dalton's face. "Sir, I protest. This man was creating a disturbance; naturally I had to—"

"How much did you pay him for your table, Chief?" Dalton asked.

"Twenty bucks, sir." The stocky man was eyeing him uncertainly, recognizing brass, not quite sure in what light his actions would appear.

"Better find room in the front row for his party," Dalton said to the headwaiter.

"I'll give him his money back. I never promised—"

"He doesn't want his money back; he wants his table." Dalton spoke quietly, smiling the while; the headwaiter glanced at him and away.

"You've got no right," he said. "I don't know who you are—"

"That can easily be rectified—if that's the way you want it."

The headwaiter glowered, turned angrily to his men, barked orders. They fanned out, leaning over diners' shoulders to murmur smooth explanations, then sliding tables sideways, making room for the sailors. The latter grinned and made carefree saluting gestures toward Dalton and Arianne.

"They're fine now," Arianne said, "but *we* can't see a thing." She craned her neck.

"Sir . . ." The stocky man was beside Dalton again. "If you'n' the lady would like to join us over at our table, you could see fine—thanks to you, sir."

"Thank you, Chief," Arianne spoke up. "We'd like to."

The floor show was fast-moving, loud, colorful. The clientele loved it. There were cheers and whistles as the tiny, elfin stripteuse doffed her final wisp and pirouetted; oiled, shaved, totally nude in a pool of blue light. One of the large men at the adjacent table, applauding enthusiastically, jostled the sailor seated inches from him.

"Watch it, Clyde," the latter called. The civilian gave him a lift of the eyebrow and turned away. A waiter, arriving with drinks for the party of six, pushed past the sailor, thrusting his rump hard against his chair as he leaned to serve the civilians. The sailor casually hooked a finger under the waistband of the waiter's trousers and upended a drink in the gap thus created. The waiter howled and leaped. One of the plump women yelped, batting ineffectually at a drink which had been precipitated into her décolletage. Two of the men jumped up, throwing down napkins, both shouting at once:

". . . devil is the meaning of this?"

". . . by God, I'll see the pack of you hoodlums jailed!"

"You and what gunboat, blubber-gut?" the offended sailor shouted across to him. The stocky CPO grabbed the sailor's arm, spoke urgently to him. The two large civilians sat down. The waiter quivered and disappeared. Arianne tittered. One of the sailors winked at her. The sailors were talking and laughing now, loudly enough to be heard over the boom of the music as a trio of tumblers spilled onto the floor and went into their routine.

One of the civilians at the next table rose, started past the table where Dalton sat. Suddenly he lurched, seemed to leap forward, crashed down on his face, overturning a table in the process. A woman screeched; the man's companions were on their feet. Waiters came hurrying; two helped up the fallen man.

"That goddamned deck-ape deliberately tripped me!" he yelled, pointing at a sailor. All four Navy men on their feet in an instant. The stocky CPO shot Dalton a conspiratorial glance. People were standing, craning their necks. Two strange sailors appeared, pushing through the press; one collided with a waiter, sending him staggering. The maître d' bustled forward, his trouble crew at his heels. Suddenly there were dozens of uniformed men confronting an equal number of Aldans, not all of whom were in waiters' dress. Dalton saw a burly man in stained kitchen whites with a cleaver gripped in his fist. He rose and stepped to the CPO's side.

"Party's over, Chief," he said. "You and your men do a fast fade."

The CPO's face was flushed, his eyes bright. "Hell, we can handle this bunch," he blurted.

Dalton gripped his arm. "Move out—now," he rapped.

The stocky man—half a head shorter than Dalton—stared at him, half-surprised, half-defiant. The headwaiter was shouting. One of the heavyweight civilians was yelling and pointing. A sailor was unobtrusively slipping a set of brass knuckles over his fist.

"Snap to it," Dalton said, "before this gets out of hand."

A sailor started past Dalton toward the nearest waiter; Dalton moved to block his way.

"Hell, whose side you on?" the man blurted. A waiter shouldered up, reaching for a sailor; Dalton tramped on his instep, rammed an elbow to his ribs, and faced the stocky man.

"Report to your ship on the double, Chief," he

growled. "If you're in any doubt, that's a direct order."

The man hesitated, then turned away, snapped something at his men. They shot hostile glances at Dalton and the waiters, then caught up their hats, grabbed their confused girls' arms, and pushed away through the crowd. The waiters stood back and let them go. The others were already turning back to the floor show.

Dalton resumed his seat. Arianne looked at him quizzically. "Very dramatic," she said sarcastically, shaking her head. "I don't understand you, Tan. First you put yourself on the spot by standing up for them; then you lost whatever good will you might have earned for yourself by turning against them. Why?"

He studied her face—patrician, intelligent, appealing. "Is it really so hard to understand?"

"Oh, I know it's a commander's job to look out for his men, and it wouldn't help their morale to be cheated in a nightclub, but you took a terrible chance, stepping in as you did. A commodore can't be mixed up in a common brawl—especially in a place like this."

"When you go in a place like this, as you put it, you're laying it on the line. Would you have had me sit by silently?"

"Yes. Why not?" She grimaced, put her hand over his. "No, I don't really mean that. I was glad you helped them. But then—" she shook her head. "Tan, don't you have any feel for the *politics* of things? The story will be all over the fleet by morning—not that you helped them, but the other part. And what good did you do? They'll go somewhere else and start a fight. They're in the mood."

"Maybe. Let's forget it. What would you like to do now?"

Arianne took a deep breath and smoothed out her face.

"Father wants to see you," she said. "I . . . think it's something important, Tan." Her eyes searched his face. "Try to . . . not to . . ."

"Not to disgrace myself?" Dalton half-smiled. "I'll do my best."

CHAPTER TWO

Senator Kelvin was waiting in his suite at the Embassy; he returned Dalton's greeting with a curt nod.

"Sit down, Dalton," he said somberly. He stared at the younger man, pushing his lips in and out. "This fleet exercise," he said abruptly, "is more important than is generally realized, even among those who're charged with the responsibility of carrying it out. Ostensibly, the purpose of the operation is to show the flag, parade our strength, and in general make the Hukk understand that we've had enough harassment. In confidence—it's not quite so simple."

Dalton waited.

"We blundered on our initial contacts with the Hukk over a century ago," Kelvin said. "We should have taken a firm line from the outset. Instead, we played the fairy godmother. We set out to uplift them; we helped them advance technologically; we taught them, even sent material aid. Then, when they trod on our toes experimentally, we failed to slap them down. Instead we were patient; we hedged. We compromised. So—naturally—they pushed again, harder. Before long, we'd reached the stage of embargo and boycott. Even that degree of response caused our Softline people to howl with indignation. Now—we reap the rewards of our flabby policies. A full-scale war of attrition—with the Hukk openly harassing our colonies, occupying our territories, preying on our commerce— and still there are those who choose to look on this aggression as mere boyish high spirits. They tell us we should accede gracefully to Hukk demands, show them our good will, and in time they'll see the error of their ways." Kelvin smacked a fist into his palm.

"Don't they realize the Hukk have grown into a full-scale menace—at our expense?" Kelvin went on. "They've duplicated our equipment, aped our organizational methods, used our own techniques against us. They're fast learners, the Hukk; let's give them full credit. And they stand in no doubt whatever where Hukk interests lie. While for our part . . . we whine and cavil and hope that somehow, some day, they'll reform and we'll all become the best of friends."

"I take it you don't have much faith in the effectiveness of the upcoming exercise," Dalton said.

"This is in total confidence, Dalton," Kelvin said. "Only the Joint Chiefs, the Council and my committee are in on it. If word got out that I'd told you—well, I'll leave it to your imagination—after you've heard it."

Dalton nodded.

"The fleet mission, insofar as the field commanders know—and that includes Admiral Starbird—is to carry out war games in Border Space. By showing the Hukk our fleet, we indicate—just subtly, you understand—that we wish they'd go away and stop making nuisances of themselves. If they interfere—they'll presumably be dealt with accordingly."

"That was my understanding, Senator."

"It's a lie—a smoke screen," Kelvin said. "Given out for the sake of fleet morale. The men will function more effectively, it's believed, if they can smell a little blood. However—Starbird carries sealed orders, to be opened on first contact. Those orders forbid him to open fire."

"There has to be more," Dalton said.

"I wish there were. The theory is, the mere sight of our fleet will send them scurrying for cover."

"Maybe—but I doubt it. They've had a taste of success. They think they have a winning combination. And if it comes to a fight, we'll be at a considerable disadvantage. If we can't return fire until—"

"Who said anything about returning fire?" Kelvin cut in hotly.

"I assumed—"

"You assumed in error! The fleet will *not open fire!* Those are the orders!" Kelvin strode to the bar in the corner of the room, poured two stiff brandies, came back, and handed one to Dalton.

"Those are the orders," he repeated.

"Are we allowed to duck?" Dalton inquired. "Or do we just sit there and absorb it?"

"According to the Softliners who're responsible for this piece of villainy," Kelvin said, "you'll be perfectly safe. The Hukk, being earnest pacifists at heart, will never be the first to fire. So if we don't fire, there'll be no battle. Q.E.D."

"Has anybody notified the Hukk that this isn't a real battle they're heading into?"

"Unfortunately, no."

Dalton swirled the brandy in his glass. "We'll be facing real, live nuclear warheads out there"—he started—

"A mere detail. After all, you're professional military men. You don't count—not to the bleeding hearts."

Dalton looked inquiringly at Kelvin. "You didn't call me here just to tell me it's hopeless."

Kelvin nodded. "I see you're thinking along the same lines I am, Dalton. That's good. It saves explanations." Kelvin went to the desk, switched on a projector. A star-chart sprang into being in midair.

"En route to rendezvous you're to give Petreac a wide berth. The Hukk have been secretly assembling squadrons of raiders there for months now. Officially we're not aware of the Hukk installations there. And you're to take up station here on the left of the fleet point.

"Pretty lines on a chart." Kelvin snorted. "But this isn't the Battle of Gettysburg. You're wide open to a flanking movement from Petreac—"

"Or from the other hot spot we don't know about, over at Leadpipe," Dalton put in.

"We're talking as if this were a battle, Dalton," Kelvin said sardonically. "It's only a propaganda maneuver, remember? They'll fold up as soon as they see the color of our money, or the whites of our eyes, or however the old saying goes. Or so the Softliners tell me. However—if by some miscalculation they happen to be wrong and the Hukk *do* jump you— prematurely . . . which they might well do if you appear to be making a feint in their direction . . . and if you should just happen to blast a few squadrons of Hukk raiders out of space *before* Starbird has time to order you to turn the other cheek . . ." Kelvin looked balefully at Dalton.

"Sounds like fun," Dalton said. "But what if Starbird takes the fleet into action after all? I won't be in a position to give him any support."

"Don't worry about that," Kelvin said. "I told you what his orders are."

"Starbird used to be a pretty tough baby. He might kick over the traces when the battle board lights up."

"Sure, he was out to make a record twenty years ago in the Belt, but he's not playing the glory game any more. He's an old man and he's got his. Admittedly you may be laying your career on the line. There'll be a board of inquiry, probably a court-martial. Possibly prison." The senator laughed silently, humorlessly. "It's curious, isn't it? A career Navy man is expected to risk his life in the line of duty—die with a slogan on his lips and all the rest of it—but to risk his precious rank and privileges by defying orders—just to save his world from a disaster —that's different, that's not part of the game."

"The hazards of war," Dalton said.

"I can't order you, of course," Kelvin said. "But if you remember what I've said—and act on it—you'll have my backing—and that of a number of powerful men. Think it over, Dalton."

"I will," Dalton said.

2

A uniformed driver was waiting for Dalton in the dark street at the foot of the Embassy drive; he jumped forward and opened the door of the big black car as Dalton came up. He was a big man with cat-like eyes, trim in his white CDT custodial uniform.

"Who ordered the car?" Dalton inquired casually.

"It's for you, sir," the driver said with a confidential smile that narrowed his cat's eyes even further.

"That's not what I asked you," Dalton said, almost carelessly.

"It's SOP, sir." The man shifted his feet, still smiling.

"You're a liar," Dalton said softly. The smile
disappeared.

"Wha—?"

Dalton came close to the man, who was as tall as
he, almost as wide.

"Who sent you here?"

The man's hand started toward his hip; Dalton took
him by the collar and slammed him against the side
of the car. Something clattered on the pavement. Dalton glimpsed an outlawed wire gun before it skittered
into the gutter. The man tried to knee him; Dalton
intercepted it. The man tried to jerk away; Dalton
rapped his head sharply against the low roof of the
car.

"You're a strong boy," he said, "but I'm lots
stronger. Start telling it."

"You can't—" the man blurted. "What is this—?"

"This is you fluffing the assignment," Dalton said,
his face six inches from the other's, "Now, for extra
points—where were you supposed to take me?"

"To . . . to the ROB."

Dalton doubled his fist and slammed a short right
hook to the driver's midriff; the man fell against him,
gagging.

"This is a nice quiet spot, chum, so we can talk un-
disturbed," Dalton said in the man's ear. "You handled that part fine. Better get started." When the man
failed to answer, Dalton took his wrist up behind him,
applied pressure. The man wailed.

"You'll break it, you son of a joy-girl!"

"Right again." Dalton twisted harder.

"I don't know his name!" the man gasped. "Big
shot—bushy white hair, gold ring—like yours."

"You're doing fine."

"There was another guy with him—small, fancy-dressed, slick black hair. Younger."

"And where are these two nice men staying?"

"I don't kno—oh! All right! The Breakwater!"

Dalton pushed the man away; he slumped against the car, sweat running down his narrow face.

"They never told me . . ." the man muttered, looking sideways at Dalton.

"Sure—all the tough guys are supposed to be on the other side," Dalton said. "Let's go. Get in."

"G-go where?"

"To the Breakwater. You've got my curiosity aroused, chum. Since you won't talk, maybe they will."

3

The Breakwater filled a four-acre lot above the beach, an uncompromising polyhedron of reflective plastic hung in giant H-frames, bright-lit, landscaped and pooled and terraced. Dalton ordered the car to a halt before the spread of air doors; an SP lieutenant hurried forward, summoned by the signaller in Dalton's pocket.

"Take this man in to the lockup." He indicated the startled driver. "Charge him with impersonating a CDT employee and theft of an official vehicle, for openers. I'll fill in the blanks later."

He went up the steps between the imported palms, bathed in green and blue floodlights, across the wide lobby to the hundred-foot reception desk.

"Mr. Lair's suite," he said.

The clerk's eyes flickered. "I don't believe—" he started.

"Neither do I," Dalton cut in. "The suite number, please. No time for protocol."

The clerk raised an eyebrow and started to turn away. Dalton's hand stopped him. The clerk looked down at the hand on his sleeve with the indignation of a matron accosted in the street.

"Sir!" he almost squeaked. "This sort of behavior is not tolerated at the *Breakwater!*" He wriggled; a door behind the desk snapped open, and a tall man with a baggy brown face eased through, apparently unhurriedly. His eyes slid past Dalton. He came over and leaned an elbow on the desk.

"Trouble?" he inquired diffidently.

"It could grow up to be, maybe," Dalton said. "But it doesn't have to."

"Tell him to unhand me," the clerk snapped; Dalton was still holding his sleeve.

"You could kind of let go Mr. Swink," the brown man said mildly. "I'm Katz, the house man."

Dalton released him. "Tell Mr. Swink to stay close, Mr. Katz. My call is confidential."

"Who was the party you was wanting to see?"

"The Undersecretary."

"If Secretary Treech was here—and I ain't saying he is—maybe he wouldn't want to be disturbed."

"Just give me the suite number. I'll find my own way up."

"Maybe I better see that ID," the brown man said. His eyes flickered over Dalton.

"You know better."

The brown man glanced at Swink. "Go sort some mail," he muttered, "and don't go pushing any buttons."

The clerk sniffed and went away. The brown man sighed and rolled an eye at Dalton.

"I got a job to do—" he started.

"The number," Dalton cut in. "Just the number—if you like the job, that is."

"You kind of throw your weight around, Cap'n," the brown man said resentfully.

"That's what weight's for."

The brown man nodded; his eyes wore a resigned look. "Suite two-two-three A," he murmured. "Watch the hard boy on the gate."

"Why? Does he do card tricks?"

"I wouldn't want no trouble," the brown man said in an aggrieved tone.

Dalton rode the lift up to the twenty-second floor. The doors hissed open on a fawn-colored foyer decorated with terra cotta urns, gilt mirrors and pale leather divans of the kind on which no one ever sat. A man was sitting on one, reading a newspaper. He gave Dalton a quick look over the top edge of it.

"Don't get up," Dalton said. "Two-two-three A, right?" He walked past the man, who came up out of his seat with a rattle of paper.

"Hold it—sir," he barked. Dalton kept going; as the man coming up behind reached for him, Dalton bent his knees, extended his right arm, and came around in a scything arc. The edge of his hand caught the man square across the jaw, crunchingly. He went back against the wall and down. Dalton took two quick steps and kicked the gun from the man's hand as it snaked out from an inside pocket.

"Naughty," Dalton said. "You forgot to ask for my engraved invitation."

The man rolled to his knees, and a door opened ten feet along the corridor. Lair, the small, dark Assistant Undersecretary of Defense whom Dalton had met over drinks that afternoon popped into view.

"What the—"

"Evening, Mr. Lair," Dalton said. The man he had felled got to his feet shakily.

"This jasper—" he started.

"What's the meaning of this, Dalton?" Lair snapped.

"I thought the Undersecretary sent for me," Dalton said. "My mistake."

Lair's face twitched. "Come inside," he said tightly, and stepped back. Dalton went past him into a hall done in powder blue and antique silver, along that to a wide, split-level living room ornate with railings, cornices, polished furniture, silks, hangings, ceramics, drapes, a corner bar. Beside a wide fireplace a bulky, big-faced man with a shock of silver-white hair perched on the edge of a vast leather chair. He watched Dalton come across the room, looked past him at Lair.

"He attacked Weaver," Lair said sharply.

"Where's that other fellow—Pratt?"

"The SPs picked him up, Mr. Undersecretary," Dalton volunteered. "Seems he stole the car he was driving. Mind if I smoke?"

The big white-haired man's face pulled down into a grim expression. "Please don't. I suppose you're wondering why I, ah, sent for you, Dalton."

Dalton looked at him evenly, not answering.

"You spent a part of the afternoon with Senator Kelvin," Treech said. "I want a full report on what took place at that meeting."

Dalton continued to look at the white-haired man. The latter's face slowly darkened.

"Well?" the elder man snapped. "Speak up! I'm not accustomed to asking subordinates twice!"

"Maybe," Dalton said, "you'd better go through the usual channels, Mr. Undersecretary."

The flush drained from the Undersecretary's face, leaving it clay-pale.

"You insolent young pup, I could have you broken for that!"

"Is that why you sent your gun-boy around?"

The elderly man made a choking sound. "You dare to speak to me as if I were some common, some cheap—"

"Why not get to the point, Mr. Undersecretary? You're too big a man to have a stroke because I didn't kiss your hand. Nobody knows but Lair, and he won't tell."

With a visible effort, the white-haired man pulled himself together. He drew a deep breath and settled himself back in his chair. He arranged his meaty features in a bland expression.

"I see I've taken the wrong tack in dealing with you, Dalton," he said in a strained voice. "I was ill advised." He shot a vengeful look at Lair. "You'd better go see to your protégé, Mr. Weaver, Jerry," he said. "And do something about Mr. Pratt, your other protégé."

When the small man had left, the older man turned a calculating gaze on Dalton. "Cigar? Drink?"

"You didn't send Pratt out to bring me over here for a drink, Mr. Undersecretary."

"You don't make a great deal of effort to be conciliatory, do you, Dalton?"

"Not much."

The older man took a breath as if fighting to control his temper.

"Does that sort of thing really work sometimes?" Dalton asked in a tone of honest curiosity.

The old man gave him a blank look. Then he suddenly laughed. He reached over and slapped Dalton's knee.

"Damn right, boy," he said briskly. "Huffing and puffing and glowering has put me where I am today.

It's almost refreshing to encounter someone who sees through it." He leaned back, suddenly sober again.

"Look here, Dalton—I'll be candid with you. There are . . . forces at work which pose a serious threat to the success of our entire Hukk policy; our Hukk strategy, I should say. Those of us who've worked for so many years toward certain large ends quite naturally don't look with favor on any hotheaded schemes designed to circumvent the fruition of that policy."

"In other words, having staked your prestige on the Softline, you're not interested in seeing it blow up in your face."

Treech looked startled. "Very well—if you find over-simplification helpful." The Undersecretary forced a smile, dropped it. "By any words, it's not to Terran advantage to see anything go awry as regards the conduct of the forthcoming arrantly provocative maneuvers."

"Why tell *me*, Mr. Undersecretary?"

"You *could* be in a key position, Dalton. You've been given an important command for the operation; almost thirty percent of our first-line weapons systems are included in your flotilla and ancillary units."

Dalton waited. The Undersecretary intertwined his fingers, steepled them, drummed them together.

"It's most unusual to entrust an officer of your rank with a responsibility of such gravity. I, ah, myself, of course was not without influence during the discussions of the appointment."

"Yes," Dalton said, "I heard you tried to sidetrack it."

Treech flushed. "Be that as it may—damn it, Dalton, you're not making this any easier for me!"

Dalton said nothing. The elderly man glared at him, shook his head, smoothed his features.

"I see you're not a man to be managed, Dalton.

Very well, I'll come to the point. Your flotilla is, in effect, an independent command. You're separately based, supplied from your own depots, operating directly out of Supreme Headquarters. To a degree, you're on your own."

"I'm under Admiral Starbird's command—"

"Bah! That old relic! Still regaling people with stories of the Belt operation in '88. He can be brushed aside like the old woman he is."

"By whom—and for what?"

"I'm coming to that. Now—you know the strategic and tactical situation we're facing. The Hukk are operating close to their supply bases, we at a distance. Their forces will be concentrated on an inner arc, contractible inward on their lines of communication under pressure. Under similar pressures our front will tend to fragment—"

"I've studied the situation, Mr. Undersecretary," Dalton interrupted gently.

"I'm not attempting to inform you of basics, merely to direct your attention to certain facts," the old man snapped. "Very well, then, under a determined attack, our forces will fall apart—break up into at least three major nuclei, about which units will rally. I refer to Borgman's command, on the east, Veidt's in the center—and your own flotilla."

Dalton nodded. "I follow you."

"I have certain information in my possession," the Undersecretary said solemnly, "which indicates that at the moment of rendezvous, Admiral Borgman will declare that old dotard Starbird incompetent and assume command. In this he will be supported by Veidt."

"Go on," Dalton said.

"The purpose of this piece of treachery," the old man said, "will be to launch an all-out attack on cer-

tain selected Hukk targets, in defiance of the departmental policy of restrained reaction."

"What targets?"

"I haven't been able to secure that information. But
they'll be selected for maximum enemy response. I
imagine the Hukk field capital at Bofors might be a
logical target for these fanatics, as well as their installations at Doon 8 and Auclaire IV and V. Targets of
no military importance—but hitting them will stir up
the Hukk like hornets."

"And of course they'll retaliate in kind."

"Exactly! For which one can't blame them. That's
what Borgman and his group are after. They *want* incidents, propaganda material. The Hukk will strike
back at every unprotected Terran site within reach—
and the public outcry will do the rest! It will be all-
out, total war!"

"And where do I enter the picture?"

"You're no fool, Dalton." The old man's eyes glittered at him. "Isn't it obvious?"

"You envision me somehow talking Borgman and
Veidt out of pulling off their coup?"

"Nonsense," the Undersecretary barked. "You
wouldn't stand a chance. They outrank you six ways
from the ace. You've got to move first, man, and relieve Starbird before they can reach him!"

4

"I have here," the Undersecretary said gravely,
producing a heavy official-blue envelope, "special orders issued directly from the Office of the Secretary of
Defense, authorizing you to assume battle command
of the fleet under the circumstances detailed herein."

He tapped the envelope with a gnarly forefinger. "Needless to say, any premature or unauthorized disclosure of the substance of this document will result in complete repudiation thereof."

"Why me?" Dalton asked. "You've got hundreds of tame admirals back at the department."

"Precisely!" the Undersecretary snorted. "Tame admirals. We need a more dynamic type for this kind of finesse, Dalton. A maverick—like yourself." He gave Dalton a hard look. "I confess I opposed your appointment—but we've sense enough to use the best tools at hand."

"Who's 'we'?"

"In addition to myself—and my Assistant Undersecretary, Lair—yes, yes, I know your opinion of the man. In part I share it myself, but he's a shrewd professional, an old government hand. He'll pull his weight. In addition, I say, there'll be a good proportion of the top echelon Naval brass, certain key legislators, and at least three Council members."

Dalton looked steadily at the older man. "You're kidding," he said.

"No, I assure you—"

"*You* might get by with it—under the Constitution, you're immune—the rest would end up on Caine Island."

"Kindly rest assured I'm not in the habit of taking blind risks. We're covered, Dalton—we're solid. There'll be no slipups—not if you carry out your part as ordered."

"What about after—when I've assumed command?"

"You know my position. Confronted with evidence of our determination, the Hukk will back off, saving face along the line, of course. Restraint is the keynote, Dalton." The Undersecretary leaned forward, fists clenched. "You've got to get us out of this without allowing open hostilities to flare up. Afterwards . . . well, there are methods of dealing with these damned aliens that don't necessitate the public eating of crow by myself and my colleagues."

"I get the picture—all but one item: What do *I* get out of all this?"

"What's that? You follow orders, Dalton—you're a career officer! Are you asking for a payoff?"

"I already have my orders, Mr. Undersecretary. They don't say anything about mutiny. You're suggesting I put my head on the block to save your political bacon—"

"To save mass loss of life, you young hound!"

"Thanks for the talk, Mr. Undersecretary." Dalton got to his feet.

"Just a minute, man! Damn it—I apologize! I'm sorry if I was offensive. I suppose I'm too accustomed to yes-men."

"Don't kid me, Mr. Undersecretary," Dalton said. "You turn it on and off like a light switch. What kind of puzzles me is that you want the kind of man who can take a couple of battle fleets away from a pair of tough old war dogs without mussing his hair—but at the same time you expect him to be docile enough to be brought in by a second-rate gun-punk and then browbeaten with some third-rate histrionics."

The elderly man waggled his hands. "I've handled you incorrectly, granted. For your part, you've caused me considerable embarrassment. Having Lair's man Pratt under the lights at SP headquarters could be awkward; you knew that when you sent him there. That wasn't necessary, Dalton. That was a piece of bravado on your part. So possibly we're both frustrated hams." He managed a genial chuckle. "I'm prepared to write off what's gone before and start afresh, without prejudice," he said in a tone of one making a concession.

"You didn't answer my question."

The old man opened his mouth as if to shout, closed it again.

"Yes. Well, it's clear that your timely action in averting disaster will not go unrecognized. I should think you'd have your two stars in no time—and after that—with the proper patronage—there's no limit to the possibilities for advancement."

"So I pull your fat out of the fire, and you get me a promotion."

"If it pleases you to put it that way."

"I'll think it over, Mr. Undersecretary."

The old man picked up the envelope and thrust it at Dalton.

"These are orders, Dalton. Official, authenticated orders. Ignore them at your peril."

"You can't speak two sentences without throwing in a threat, can you, Mr. Undersecretary?"

"By God, Dalton, too much is dependent on the subtle and precise handling of this affair! I can't make an issue of Borgman and Veidt's plans, because I have no solid proof. I can't openly demand Starbird's relief, or I'll have the Hardliners down on me like a plague. This is the only way—and you're the only man I can entrust it to." The white-haired man paused, looked calculatingly at Dalton.

"Unless, possibly, you're opposed on ideological grounds to preventing a major war. Just where do you stand, Dalton?"

"I'm not a joiner, Mr. Undersecretary."

"You must have opinions, What's your alignment? Hardline or Softline?"

"I hadn't heard I had to make a choice."

The old man shook his head, his eyes fixed on Dal-

ton. "I'm handing you the opportunity of a lifetime,
man," he said softly. "You pull this off and you can
name your spot. Fail—but I'll leave that to your imagination. You can call that a threat if you like."

5

A pallid, jowly, youngish man with carefully
combed hair and a beautifully cut suit which almost
disguised his developing paunch was waiting in the
anteroom to Dalton's suite when he returned to the
ROB.

"Ah, there, Commodore Dalton," he said in a tone
of leisurely gratification. "I hope you'll excuse my intrusion—"

"What if I don't?" Dalton said. "What do you want
tonight, Passwyn?"

"Why, just a social call, I happened to be passing,
and—"

"Let's skip over the rituals, OK? I'm tired. I have a
big day tomorrow. We're starting a war, remember?
I understand you're here unofficially, and anything
you say will be denied by the Embassy if I mention
it in polite society. Now that that's out of the way,
what do you want?"

"You've no need to be rude, Dalton—"

"Commodore Dalton to you, Passwyn; remember
your manners. A Second Secretary ranks with and
after a light commander. Get to the point. I've had a
full day's pussyfooting since lunch."

"Well, if that's your attitude . . ." Passwyn rose,
plucked his briefcase from the seat beside him. When
Dalton made a move, he paused. "I had in mind dis-

cussing a matter of some advantage to you, but if you don't wish to hear of it . . ."

Dalton looked at him and said nothing.

"Still, I don't wish to take umbrage unduly," Passwyn said, and used a tight little smile. "In a matter of such delicacy—"

"Spit it out or swallow it, Passwyn. What's your deal? I do a sneak into Hukk Imperial Battle HQ and swipe the war plans, and you'll put in a good word for me with the greens committee?"

"Flippancy is hardly called for, I think, Commodore."

"Good night, Passwyn. Nice of you to drop around. Come again tomorrow; I'll be gone then."

"Look here, Dalton—I have to talk to you. May we go inside?"

"Next thing you'll be expecting a dinner invitation. Come on in; I can give you five minutes. Don't mind me if I hum a little tune while you're talking."

The diplomat followed silently. In the small but handsomely appointed living room he dumped his briefcase on a low table, unstrapped it, and took out a sheet of paper.

"I have here," he stated importantly, "the names of certain Naval personnel in whom we have an interest. Now, I want to know what you can tell me about these individuals: their attitudes, reliability, political orientation, and so on." He handed the paper across. Dalton glanced at it.

" 'Admiral Veidt,' " he read. " 'Admiral Borgman. Commodore Stein.' Distinguished officers, all of them. Fine records; plenty of the right decorations—"

"Yes, yes, I'm familiar with all that. What I'm after is the, ah, offbeat item. The, er, little personal observation which may in the end be more revealing than the public character."

"The dirt, in other words. Well, let's see: I heard a rumor that Borgman had five drinks at the club one night when he was an ensign, and knocked three teeth out of the bartender's jaw when he refused to serve him another. Took plenty to hush that one up; and I hear Stein has secret links with the New Zion movement—and—"

"Please, Commodore Dalton—don't be arch. You know what I'm after."

"You want the real stuff, eh? 'Which way will they jump in the crunch?' "

"An index of reliability, shall we say?" Passwyn suggested. "One hears so many rumors . . . the opinions of an insider such as yourself would be of great value in coming to a realistic assessment."

"How much value?"

Passwyn smiled coolly. "I feel quite confident in suggesting that at any time you felt impelled to resign from active military duty, a place could be found for you in the Corps, Commodore."

"I'm kind of miffed your bunch saw fit to handle this at Second Secretary level," Dalton said. "I'd think I'd at least have the Counsellor's personal attention."

"I'm sure Counsellor Spradley will be happy to see you, but of course in these matters one must observe a certain circumspection."

"So I give you the lowdown on my colleagues, and you set aside a soft berth for me at some nice little consulate general somewhere."

Passwyn murmured something, smiling sleekly.

"What are you really after?" Dalton asked abruptly.

"Why, I'm sure that's not for you—or myself, for that matter—to question. Corps policy is to be fully informed on all phases of the developing situation. This is merely one small piece in the larger mosaic of—"

"What have you heard about Veidt and Borgman, say?"

"I'm not at liberty to discuss—"

"Better change that. I want to know what I'm getting into."

Passwyn looked grave. "Very well. Under the circumstances . . . I can tell you that we've had indications—from generally reliable sources—"

"Paid informers in the ranks, you mean?"

"Something of the sort," Passwyn said severely. "Indications, as I was saying, of some sort of intramural coup in the making. A plan to carry out a shuffle of command personnel at a critical moment. Naturally, the Corps must keep abreast of such developments in order to assume an appropriate posture."

Dalton nodded. "I see. You don't care who wins, but you want to be ready to jump in the right direction."

"It would hardly be to Terran advantage, Commodore, if the *Corps Diplomatique* were caught off-base, so to speak," Passwyn said stiffly.

"So this little survey will help you decide what documents to plant where, so that afterward you can prove you were backing the winner all along, eh?"

"I'm not at all sure I like the tenor of your comments, Commodore. You seem to be imputing some sort of discreditable motives to the Corps—"

"What about a couple of items outside the Navy? Legislative branch stuff, for example—or maybe even a little cabinet-level involvement . . . ?"

Passwyn's expression smoothed out into a look of bland courtesy. "I think you'd find the Corps interested, Commodore. The scope of our duties—our responsibilities, that is to say—"

"How much?"

"How, er, much?" Passwyn looked disconcerted.

"What are you offering? Come on, Passwyn, open up. You didn't expect me to come across for free, did you?"

"I think," the diplomat said carefully, "that, based on the importance of the specific items—after verification, of course—"

"You think? Didn't they give you any instructions when they sent you out on your scavenger mission?"

Passwyn paled, then blushed. "I didn't come here to be insulted," he said in a strangled voice.

"I didn't invite you up here, Passwyn. You can leave anytime."

Passwyn looked startled. "Leave? You haven't yet —we haven't yet—my instructions . . . look here—I can't go back empty-handed!"

"Sorry to disappoint you. I've got a bad memory for gossip."

"But see here." Passwyn was on his feet. "I've confided in you, Dalton—laid my cards on the table. I naturally assumed—"

"Better hope your boss doesn't find out you gave away all that weight without any payoff. So long, Passwyn. Give my regards to the boys in the sewer."

"Why, you deliberately deceived me—led me on— you—!"

"Better stop there. Just trip the night latch on your way out."

Passwyn, pale of face and with trembling fingers, stuffed his papers back in the briefcase.

"One thing," he snapped, jerking the straps tight. "What's passed between us is confidential—of the highest classification. Any irresponsible talk on your part, and—I anticipate an even earlier curtailment to your so-called career than even your lack of the minimum graces would warrant. Do I make myself, er, clear?"

"If you make it any clearer, I'll have to break your jaw."

"They told me you were a fool," Passwyn said, edging around the end of the table. "In view of your military record, I doubted it. But now I understand. You're a fool of a particular type—"

"Much too particular—of who I spend my evenings with. Scram, Passwyn. You're overloading the air conditioning."

"The day will come when you'll wish you had a friend in the CDT."

"That's a hell of a thing to wish on a friend. A nice stretch on the rock pile, now—or pumping out cesspools—"

Passwyn was at the door. "I'll see you broken for this, Dalton," he said, and ducked as Dalton took a step toward him.

After the diplomat had gone, Dalton stood for a while by the window, staring down at the spreading lights of the old city.

"Hell," he said at last, softly, to himself.

Then he switched on the repeater tank that had been installed in the room. For the next three hours he studied the developing tactical relationships in space, near Piranha, tapping keys to code in variations on fleet disposition, setting up one contingent situation after another, noting times, distances, relationships, alternatives in the event the planned maneuvers flared into open hostilities.

CHAPTER THREE

Arianne accompanied Dalton to the port the following morning.

"Be careful, Tan," she said as the big car pulled to a stop before the entry to the operations complex. "There's more to this big parade than just simply showing the flag. I don't know what's going on—but Dad's very tense about it. Keep your eyes open. And Tan—keep your mouth closed when you have a chance—just as a favor to me?"

He smiled and kissed her on the mouth.

"Goodbye for now, girl. If I see my mouth coming open I'll stuff a foot in it."

"Just be sure it's yours and not the admiral's."

The car door slammed; he had a last glimpse of a pert face, the wave of a gloved hand, and a lingering trace of subtle perfume as the car gunned away.

A harassed junior officer met him inside. He spent

the next two hours before the big log screens in the dispatch center, making the final check-list.

"If we've forgotten the stuffed eggs, it's not your fault, Sam," he said to the log officer at last. "I'm off, ready or not."

"Give 'em hell, Commodore." The officer shook his hand. "Or whatever it is Command intends to give 'em," he added, looking queryingly at Dalton.

"Yeah," Dalton said. "Keep the powder dry, just in case."

A ramp car drove him swiftly out to his flagship, a specially equipped light destroyer of a hundred kilotons. A Deck Police lieutenant in black combat gear checked him aboard. The vessel's captain, Darcy, met him at the entry port. He was young for his rank and looked as fresh and alert as if he had not been on continuous duty for the preceding forty-eight hours readying his command for space.

They rode up together to the command deck, a circular room packed with the elaborate communications and control installations necessary to enable the small ship to function as a mobile Battle HQ.

"Don't worry, George, I won't be breathing down your neck," Dalton said. "I'm just along for the ride."

"Sorry if I've got my back up, Tan. I guess the commodore's got to ride somewhere. Better you on my bridge than Volcano Veidt."

Dalton shook hands with the deck staff, glanced over the last-minute status read-outs.

"Everything's G," he said. "Lift off any time you like, George."

A special seat had been installed for him, above and behind the three command couches occupied by the captain, engineer and navigator. There was the brief rattle of the automated countdown, the rising whine of pumps, the faint trembling, the first touch of pressure that swiftly grew until Dalton's vision blurred and his pulse roared in his ears.

Then the abrupt down-whining wail of sound as acceleration slacked off to a steady .7 G.

"You climb out as if you were still jockeying F-250s," Dalton commented as Darcy elevated his chair and swung around to face him. "What's your EET to rendezvous?"

"Eight and forty, plus or minus three. I'll refine that as soon as we're lined up." The captain gave Dalton a slightly frowning smile. "The flotilla's APOAF, full strength. Even Hunneker got his bucket out of hock in time to join up. Twenty-seven fighting ships, all set and raring to go." He looked at Dalton inquiringly.

"So I heard."

Darcy laughed, not as if overwhelmed with mirth. "I know; I suppose you spent the last hour double-checking the double-checkers over at Log."

"Two."

"This is the first operation of this scale I've ever been in on," Darcy said, rubbing his chin, "even if it is only a maneuver in force."

"It's the first any of us has been in on."

"Well, sure . . . that's right, I suppose, come to think of it. . . ." Darcy looked sideways at Dalton. "Sort of an unusual fleet disposition, eh, Tan? Ninety percent of the Navy's hardware all strung out in line astern like a Flag Day parade. Kind of, ah, unconventional, wouldn't you say?"

" 'Foolish' is the word you're searching for, isn't it, George?"

"Well—you said it, not me. But—yeah. Maybe 'stupid' would be closer. For God's sake, Tan—we'll be sitting ducks! Those Hukk heavies could hit us on either flank and roll us up like a rag rug!"

"You must be mixed up, George. This is just a little show of strength, remember? Not even that, really: just a ceremonial occasion—"

"What do those balloon-brains back at SH think the Hukk are—a bunch of Cub Scouts?" Darcy demanded. "Those babies are tough, smart, and not a damn bit bashful!"

"Tsk. That's warlike talk, George."

Darcy hitched himself forward in his seat. "There's got to be more to this operation than meets the eye, Tan. Even I can figure that out." He was watching Dalton's face for a clue to his reaction.

"There are several possibilities that come to mind," Darcy went on. "One—surprise orders, to be sprung on us in the next hour or two, breaking up this *kaffeklatsch* and dispersing the fleet on specific interdiction missions."

"It's a possibility—I suppose," Dalton said.

"Two—instead of the flotilla taking up position on Veidt's left, we turn and sprint for a preselected target—or targets—inside Hukk space: Arjak, for example—and knock out their so-called observatory; or Inek, and that cozy little meteorological station they're so proud of—and if it isn't sitting on top of the biggest munitions stockpile this side of Fortress Luna, I'll eat the braid off my second-best mess dress blues."

"Could be," Dalton conceded.

"Or," Darcy continued, "this whole thing may be the biggest sleight of hand since the Russians pulled out of Africa. There's no flotilla out there, just a bunch of ghost-bogies for my comm boys—and the Hukk—to play with—and the real action will be fought in six other places. But then, I don't suppose you'd be here." Darcy rubbed his chin again and looked doubtful.

"And maybe," Dalton suggested, "the whole thing is a fire drill to see whether some of our bright young men like George Darcy have bubbles in their domes from too much shore time and female admiration."

Darcy shook his head and grinned. "Negative, Commodore. You'd be the last man in the Navy to ride shotgun on a check ride—or tell me if you were."

"How about this one," Dalton said. "It's a neat switch by the Hardliners: they conned the Softliners into sponsoring a dress parade—in the interest of peace at greatly reduced prices; but it's all a gimmick to get the fleet in space, armed, fueled, and manned at full battle levels. Once unleashed, the dogs of war go for the throat—"

"My God, Tan—you don't mean—" Darcy broke off and looked sheepish. "No, of course you don't mean. Whatever you know, you naturally can't tell—until the right moment."

"For your peace of mind, George, my intention at this time is to make the rendezvous, just as advertised."

"And then?"

"You know the published operational directive, George."

"It doesn't make any sense, Tan," Darcy said in a suddenly more intent tone. "This is not the way to use a space fleet, for God's sake! Our ships were designed to operate as independent forces, with the mission of policing our trade lanes and chasing down the occasional rogue bogey. Massing our force this way makes no sense at all. Any Navy man can see that; the brass must know we know that. This has to be a feint of some kind—and the Hukk know it too!"

"Nevertheless, the latest fleet advisory reported the Hukk still seem to be concentrating off Piranha."

Darcy nodded. " 'Seem' is the operative word, maybe. What if *they're* stacking a ghost fleet out there?

They know as much about hoking LR detectors as we do."

"Why would they do that?"

"What are you doing, Tan—leading me to some conclusion? OK, I'll go along. The Hukk would derive obvious advantages from hoaxing us into a counteraction at Piranha, while they quietly slide their real fleet around left end into the clear."

"But they couldn't maintain the deception long enough to do them any real good. Wherever they go, we can follow. We've got faster ships and better detectors."

"We'd spot it as soon as we got within AGAG range —half a parsec with these new sets," Darcy conceded. "But by then they could be halfway to damn near any place. They could hit any target in the sector!"

"Slow down, George. As you were pointing out a moment ago, a space fleet isn't a troop of cavalry. So —they dash in and hit Boge, say—or plaster Alpha— or any other nice, defenseless target. What does that buy them?"

"Well. . . ."

"That would be a patsy play—and the Hukk are too shrewd for that. They know Terran politics: we'd have all the excuse the Hardliners want to open up on them with everything we've got—and the Softliners would have the ground cut from under their feet. Our space attack capability would be intact and our danders up. And the Hukk know that in a toe-to-toe slugging match, we'd win."

Darcy rubbed his chin again. "So what does that leave us? The fleet? Even lined up like targets on the range, that's still a lot of firepower to tackle cold turkey. At best, they'd be hurt—bad."

"So—maybe they intend to sit tight like good little

boys and be intimidated, just the way we planned," Dalton suggested.

"Nuts—you and I both know better. But—damn it, Tan, I can't for the life of me see what they *do* have in mind—or us, either!"

2

Dalton's rendezvous with his flotilla was made on schedule; he immediately called a captains' conference via closed screen. Twenty-six line captains of the Navy looked out at him, waiting.

"You gentlemen know the background of the present maneuvers," Dalton said, "but I'll briefly outline the salient points. For the past three years our friends the Hukk have been pecking away at our shipping and colonies, getting bolder as we've refrained from hitting back. In the last year, we've begun to take certain limited preventive measures, purely of a restraining and nonretaliatory nature. Six weeks ago the Hukk were observed to be massing heavy units in the vicinity of Piranha. The decision was taken to exercise the fleet out in that direction as a subtle warning to the Hukk that we have muscle if we care to use it."

Dalton paused for the throat clearing and position shifting to die away.

"So much for recent history. We're here as a part of the force which presumably will convince the Hukk by its appearance that further adventures at our expense would be a mistake."

"What if they don't bluff quite that easily?" a square-faced man demanded. Dalton recognized him as Hawkins, a capable man whose vociferous Hardline sentiments had cost him promotion.

"That's just one of a number of possibilities," Dalton said. "I don't propose to go into all of them here and now. Our orders are to proceed to fleet rendezvous with Admiral Starbird and the Blue and Orange fleets at GL 284/980/05." He paused. "Naturally, under certain circumstances those orders are subject to change."

There was a stir among the listening officers, this time not expressive of boredom.

"I can't tell you right now precisely what action may be necessitated in response to the developing situation," Dalton said in a tone which seemed to imply that he himself was well aware of anticipated developments. "But I'm sure that I can depend on each of you for prompt and competent execution of whatever orders I may issue in the next few hours, however unexpected they may be. Captain Hunneker," he went on without pause, "I have special instructions for you. Tight channel, please."

Hunneker came into vivid full color; the other captains registered various expressions, their black and white images emphasizing their exclusion from the privileged communication between their commodore and one of their number.

"Hunneker, I'm not satisfied with the battle worthiness of your command. Kindly turn back to Boge for depot maintenance."

"But—Captain Dalton—Commodore, I mean—my ship—"

"That's an order, Hunneker. You'll maintain strict and total communication silence en route, including responses to any ostensible signals from SFH or Fortress Luna."

"Commodore, I personally inspected—"

"There will be one, and only one exception to my order regarding communications blackout," Dalton went on. "You'll deploy full LR detector screens as soon as you're outside range of fleet interference. In the event you pick up a trace—*any* trace whatever of activity in your sector—you'll immediately flash me a code 705 on a tight beam which you'll hold on my marker beacon for that purpose. Clear?"

"Clear enough," Hunneker growled. He was ten years senior to Dalton and could not forget that he had commanded TSA *Awesome* when Dalton had been second signals officer aboard her.

"I don't want any misunderstandings, or any variations from this instruction, Captain," Dalton said evenly. "We're under combat conditions—technically —and I needn't remind you that there may be aspects of the situation I'm not at liberty to disclose to you."

"Aye, sir," Hunneker said glumly. "Return to Boge it is."

Dalton switched Hunneker out and gave a final word to the remaining twenty-five commanders:

"Every unit will maintain full LR coverage at extreme range. I want immediate notification of *any* contact, no matter how questionable. That's all, gentlemen."

Darcy gave Dalton a questioning look as he concluded the conference hookup. "Kind of tough on Hunneker," he said diffidently. "He's never forgotten he was your CO in *Old Awful*—"

"I know," Dalton said. "Better up anchor, George. We don't want to be eating their dust."

3

Dalton's flotilla rushed toward the designated rendezvous point with the main force under Admiral Starbird, twenty hours away at full fleet acceleration. Darcy went below for a long-deferred rest. Dalton stayed on the bridge, watching the LR screens, occasionally tapping out a query to the situation computer via the console beside his chair, then brooding over the charts displayed in response on his small repeater screen. Among the crew, the initial sense of excited anticipation faded to the boredom of a long, uneventful run. The hours passed. Darcy came back up, looking more tired after his rest than before.

"I've been thinking about this thing, Tan," he said, "and I think maybe I've got it."

A light winked on Dalton's console. He punched the *Ready to Receive* button.

"It's a put-up job, a charade, pure show-biz," Darcy said. "Our bigwigs and the top Hukk leaders have gotten together—"

"Hold it," Dalton snapped. The green Xmit light was on.

"Operational Urgent, Hunneker to Commodore," a tinny voice came from the plug in Dalton's ear. "Reporting unidentified formation; type, designation unknown; proceeding on course 365/678/02 at liner velocity."

"How long have you had them under observation?" Dalton cut in.

There was a twenty-second transmission lag, during which the voice droned on, giving additional statistical information on the sighting.

"Ah—approximately one half hour," the answer to his question came. "Continuing analysis of route elements indicates application of .87 G deceleration—"

"Put Hunneker on," Dalton snapped.

". . . commencing at oh-six-nine-three standard, and increasing to value of .94 after four plus point oh-three minutes of blast. . . ."

"What's up, Tan?" Darcy asked; he and the other personnel on deck were aware that a transmission was incoming, but could not hear the exchange.

Dalton didn't answer. The droning voice had cut off

as Dalton's last instruction arrived. A moment later Hunneker's heavy voice reported.

"Why wasn't this sighting reported to me immediately?" Dalton asked the older man.

"It *was,* within a matter of minutes. It's nothing but a utility vessel convoy inbound for maintenance at Luna—"

"Is it? I was told there was no ID."

"Well—what else could it be? I wasn't aware you wanted to be troubled with trivia—"

"You're relieved. Report yourself under arrest in quarters. Put Captain Smith on.'"

Hunneker sputtered and went silent. A new voice came on, crisp, but diffident.

"Commander Smith here—"

"Captain Smith, you're in command now. Send Hunneker below. I want a continuous full-coverage input on the formation now inbound for Luna on a converging track with you. In particular, I want specific mass/ratio figures on each unit, emission analyses, maneuver elements and anything else you can get with a full-spectrum IW bounce. Close at gate velocity to extreme evasion range and dog them. Full battle alert, all defensive drills in effect. And watch out for inbound fire. Got that straight?"

"On tape, sir—but—I don't understand. This sounds as if we were closing on a hostile assault formation—"

"I'm proceeding on that assumption, Captain. Execute—and keep those tapes turning with full programmed input to my computer wave-length." Dalton whirled to Darcy. "Run a new SA including the data coming in from Red three-oh. Keep it updated at twenty-second intervals. And give me a flotilla linkup —double GUTS priority!"

Darcy nodded curtly and rapped out orders. In

seconds twenty of the subordinate captains were on screen; in five more seconds all were present.

"Flotilla maneuver," Dalton rapped. "Emergency course change to 378/594/09. Fleet emergency acceleration. Double Red alert status. Execute!" He switched off, turned to Darcy.

"That means you too, Captain!"

"Aye, sir!" Darcy broke his momentary paralysis, snapped out the necessary orders. Lights dimmed as full power went to the massive inertial attitude regulators. Giant pressures—like the sucking of an invisible undertow, Dalton thought through the red haze of acceleration—pulled at him. Lights winked and flashed across the boards; something shattered with a sharp, metallic tinkle. A loose object skittered across the canted deck. Dalton's stomach protested, tightening as the drag crossed the horizontal, tugging him upward now—or was he inverted, and falling toward the ceiling? He hung on and endured. . . .

The pressure slackened; his seat was under him again. Across the circular room, a female nav aide was retching, but still punching keys with machinelike accuracy. The speaker in Dalton's ear was rattling out strings of figures. He flicked it off, knowing that the same data, encoded, was flowing into the flagship's battle computer.

"What the hell, Commodore?" Darcy said. He looked pale and shaken. "This bucket hasn't been stood on her beam ends like that since her shakedown. What's going on?"

"Look at the readout." Dalton poked a button. His screen winked, and an illuminated Sector triagram appeared, with the flotilla indicated as a tiny cluster of winking red dots at the center. Terra was a green circle nearly off screen to the right, Luna a green dot beside it; major nav beacons showed as steady amber points. Starbird's force, the Orange and Blue fleets, almost at rendezvous now, were flashing dots to the left, the Hukk concentration awaiting them a blinking yellow point just beyond them. The unknown vessels sighted by Hunneker, indicated by a glowing pink star, occupied a position somewhat closer to Luna than Dalton's flotilla.

"Feed Hunneker's calculated position on screen as a white blip and track him," Dalton ordered the ship's computer. "And display the bogie's track as recorded and back-projected for one-hour periods."

The white blip appeared, blinking approximately halfway between Dalton's position and Luna. A pink arrow flashed into existence behind the pink star, describing a gentle arc that extended up toward galactic zenith, showing the route the unidentified ships had followed.

"What is it, Commodore?" Darcy asked, staring at the pink indication. "It has to be our stuff, that close to Luna—"

"Replot that backtrack," Dalton ordered, his command going to the situation computer three decks below. "Assume maxac from a previous position screened from our then-fix by Dongen's Cluster."

The broken pink arrow disappeared, reformed, stuttering back, curving to the point indicated.

"Commodore," Captain Smith said, "I don't understand it, but the emission analysis matches my handbook description of the Hukk standard drive." He sounded astonished.

"All right," Dalton said, "fine down your detectors and get some specific data. I want to know exactly what's out there."

"I'll do all I can, sir," Smith said. A moment later he resumed transmission. "Commodore, I get an IFF code bounce off the lead element that says it's the Hukk medium cruiser *Chaka*."

"Ye gods," Darcy spoke up, "I've heard of that tub; it's Admiral Saanch'k's flagship. The Hukk that blew a hole through our Belt defensive screen twenty years ago. He's a blood-and-guts combat man. What's *he* doing cruising around Luna with a flock of side boats?"

"I believe you'll find those side boats are at least medium-cruiser weight," Dalton said.

"I can confirm that," Smith said. "At least two heavy battlewagons, and nothing less than a 10,000 tonner in the lot."

"Thirteen hours," Dalton said. "Cute enough. They maneuvered to keep the midget cluster between them and us until we were out of detector range, and then peeled off for Luna. Now they're moving in, screened from Terra by Luna."

"What would a Hukk task force be doing on the loose—not more than sixteen hours off Terra—"

"Just what you think they'd be doing—looking for trouble. Let's see if we can't find some for them."

"And that's why you sent Hunneker back: to watch for them. Tan, how in hell did you know—"

"I didn't, but there aren't too many targets that would be worth their while."

"But we agreed a strike would be insane—"

"Not Terra. Luna."

"The fortress? That's even crazier! Why tackle a fortified position with a juicy undefended target right next door?"

"Sure, Luna's fortified—but the fleet's away—remember? If the Hukk throw in their heaviest stuff in a determined attack, they can take Luna—forts, ammo dumps, big guns and all. It wasn't designed to withstand any major attack, just to stand off raiders and hit-and-runs."

"Good God, Tan—you think they can actually do it? If they grab Luna—but what then? What good will it do them?"

"Tactically, none at all. But strategically—everything. I'm talking political strategy, of course. There they'll sit, having snatched the most publicized military installation since the Maginot Line right under our noses. We'll be staring up the muzzles of our own guns, and they'll have scored a major point in the game."

"Yes—but it's a suicide mission. They'll be surrounded—cut off—"

"So what?" Dalton said. "Once they're in possession, we can't oust them by massive frontal assault—not with fifteen thousand Terran hostages there. And knowing Hukk capabilities in living off the land, I doubt if we can starve 'em out. So—we'll have to talk 'em out—and most of the talking will be on their terms."

"Damn! Who'd have thought they had the . . . the sheer audacity—not to mention the astuteness—"

"Nobody ever said the Hukk were stupid, or timid either."

"So—they've made suckers of all of us. There's not enough combat capability on Terra now to fight off one first-line firewagon—and—" Darcy broke off. "Ye gods, Tan—Terra doesn't even know about it—or Luna! Unless you've notified them . . . ?"

"Not yet."

"I don't get it, Tan," Darcy said, studying the triagram. "You've thrown us into an intercept course—and we can just about meet 'em at the door for all the good that'll do us. You're not thinking of twisting hell-for-leather Saanch'k's tail, are you? Remember, he's

not one of their desk admirals. He's their number one
gun boy."

"I don't have much choice, George. I have to work
with what's at hand."

"But what about the fleet? Starbird—"

An override signal squawked; fleet command screen
one glowed suddenly. The grim visage of Admiral
Veidt glowered down at the room that was suddenly
silent, except for the rattling of the print-outs.

"Where do you think you're going, Dalton?" the
senior admiral inquired in his sharp, surprisingly
high-pitched voice. He stared unwinking out of the
screen, waiting for an answer to a question he clearly
considered unanswerable.

"Glad you called, Admiral," Dalton said evenly. "I
was about to request a conference command hookup."

Veidt opened his mouth, closed it again. What Dalton was saying had apparently just penetrated his pre-
occupation with what he had called to say.

"I'm not interested in excuses, Dalton," Veidt
barked. "Resume your original course at once—"

"Darcy, raise Admiral Borgman and Admiral Starbird for me," Dalton turned away to say.

"You'll give me your undivided attention, sir!"
Veidt roared from the screen.

"Cut the sound on screen one," Dalton said curtly.
A junior communications officer gave him a startled
look and complied. For a moment, Veidt's face
worked in silent rage; then it winked out.

"Use emergency override if you have to," Dalton
advised the communications man. A moment later the
surprised face of Admiral Borgman appeared on screen
two.

"What the devil's this? Oh, it's you, Dalton—
what—"

"Please stand by, sir. I have a call in for Admiral Starbird on a four-way."

"What's going on, Dalton? Saw your course change. Better have some good answers ready—"

"Sir," the technician said, "I have Admiral Starbird's exec. He says—"

"Tell him I want the admiral—full triple A crash priority!"

"What's this all about?" Borgman demanded. "Is there something I wasn't advised of—"

"Commodore Dalton." The reedy voice of the elderly supreme admiral spoke from screen three. "You wished to speak to me?"

"I do, sir. I also request Admiral Veidt's presence on a four-way."

"I assume you have some adequate explanation, Commodore." The old man's eye fixed Dalton severely.

"I do, sir," Dalton said, and waited. Starbird turned his head aside and spoke. A moment later Veidt's irate face came onto screen three.

"Gentlemen," Dalton said, "I've detected the presence of a hostile strike force over ten-light hours inside the Home Space Interdict Line. I've changed course to make the interception—"

"You're out of your mind, Dalton," Veidt snapped. "Admiral," he addressed Starbird, "I recommend this man be relieved at once and his force directed to join the fleet as previously ordered."

"Well, I don't wish to take hasty action, Dan. What—"

"You're seeing things, Dalton," Borgman said. "No Hukk force could have slipped past my pickets. And if they had—"

"They never came near your pickets, Admiral. They obviously planned this one well in advance and slipped the units into position behind Dongen's Cluster one at a time over a period of weeks, well before the present maneuver was ordered—"

"Poppycock! You've lost your senses, Dalton," Veidt bellowed. "Darcy! I'm placing you—"

"Admiral Starbird is in command, as I recall, Admiral," Dalton cut in. "I suggest you listen to the rest. I estimate I'll make contact with the enemy at oh-nine-four plus twelve—"

"Starbird, will you act—or shall I?" Veidt spoke up.

"Commodore Dalton—gentlemen—kindly keep calm. You say you have a definite ID on a hostile force, Commodore?"

"Not for the record, Admiral—I'm still running trace analyses—but I'm willing to commit myself to the assumption."

"That's enough," Borgman snapped. "Veidt's right. Admiral, I concur in his proposal that Dalton be relieved at once."

"Commodore Dalton," Starbird said, his voice showing a slight quaver, "I can appreciate your zeal in proposing pursuit of what you believed to be a hostile force, but that in no way excuses your abrogation of a fleet operational order. You will accordingly resume your previous course at once, and proceed to fleet rendezvous. I'll see you aboard my flagship as soon as you've reported your command in position."

"One moment, please," Dalton said sharply as the elderly officer turned away from the screen. "Under the circumstances I have no choice but to invoke provisional orders in my possession."

"Provisional orders—from where . . . ?" Starbird wondered aloud, gazing in perplexity at his junior.

"Direct from the office of the secretary," Dalton said. He took from an inner pocket the blue envelope handed to him by Undersecretary Treech, broke the seal, unfolded the documents inside.

"Under the authority vested in me by the Secretary of the Armed Forces," he said formally, "I hereby assume temporary command of the combined fleets. Admiral Starbird, you are relieved, sir; I respectfully request that you stand by in an advisory capacity. Admiral Veidt—" He broke off as the latter officer uttered a bellow at which the technician cut the sound back to a level which reduced the irate man's yells to twitterings.

"Gentlemen!" Starbird's voice crackled suddenly. "Silence! Commodore Dalton, it's quite clear that even if the alleged orders you claim to have received did in fact exist, under the circumstances there would be no possible method of authentication—"

"Correction, sir. Please refer to your Special Order number 1208. You'll find it includes an authentication code."

Over his subordinate admiral's protests, Starbird ordered his security officer to produce the sealed Special Order.

"Very well," he said a moment later. "I'm in possession of an authentication code, Commodore." The old face looked keenly at Dalton. "If you can match it . . ."

"Red pigeon nine," Dalton said. "Four X over two. Bar space bar, double star six-one."

"Key it in, Lieutenant," Starbird ordered his aide. There was a pause.

"Confirm," the aide's voice said off screen. Starbird looked startled. Borgman and Veidt each started to speak but checked as Starbird's voice cut through:

"Very well, Commodore Dalton, I have no choice but to accept your orders. This entire exchange has been placed in the record, of course, and will be subject to minute scrutiny at a hearing in due course—"

"Belay that," Veidt spoke up. "Starbird, I'm declaring you incompetent and assuming command. I don't know what you're up to, Dalton—what kind of half-baked coup or sellout you're mixed up in—but—"

"Admiral Veidt, you're not tracking," Dalton cut in. "All previous plans are off. Any other ideas you may have had—about a change in command, for example—are superseded by my instructions. I hope I'm making myself perfectly clear."

Veidt looked uncertain for the first time. "What would *you* know—" He stalled.

"Ask Undersecretary Treech the next time you see him," Dalton said.

There was a momentary silence. Borgman cleared his throat.

"Well, Veidt," he said, "we certainly can't buck an authenticated DI. Obviously there's more to this man than we'd anticipated. I don't like it any better than you do—and I'll make that fact known in the correct quarter—but—"

"Gentlemen, I don't have time now to discuss this at length," Dalton cut in. "You'll proceed to rendezvous as previously ordered. Total communications silence will be observed until further orders, with the exception of normal interfleet communications. All appearance of normality must be maintained. My flotilla is still out of detector range of the dummy Hukk fleet—"

"Dummy fleet . . . ?" Borgman broke in.

"You're about to rendezvous with half a dozen or so echo-transmitter barges," Dalton said.

"Just a minute, Dalton," Borgman cut in, "where'd you get *that* information?"

"While we're flexing our muscles at nothing," Dalton

went on, ignoring Borgman, "the real Hukk fleet is on course for a raid on Luna Base."

"Luna! Poppycock!" Veidt yelled.

"What proof of this do you have, Dalton?" Borgman demanded. "Damn it, man—if there's a grain of truth in what you're saying, we should throw everything we've got into a counterstrike!"

"Negative. If you break off now, they'll know they've been spotted; but they don't know my position, and by the time they realize I'm not coming up into line, it'll be too late."

"Without your flotilla, the fleet will be seriously understrength," Borgman said. "What's to stop them from hitting us while we're sitting here in parade-ground formation—"

"They want a propaganda victory, not a lot of useless casualties."

"Look here, Dalton," Veidt blurted. "Suppose we grant that you've spotted something: your correct course of action is to make your report and await orders. This is a matter for supreme command decision!"

"No time for that, Admiral. . . . That's all the conversation, gentlemen! You're moving into the fringe of the Hukk communications radius. Carry on and keep your fingers crossed." Dalton cut the screens.

Darcy looked a trifle pale under his lamp tan; his expression was that of a man at the scene of a disaster. "You kind of shook 'em up, Tan—"

"Hold a monitor on the dummy Hukk position: I want a continuous readout on the main fleet dispositions. At the first sign of any variation from the script, advise me at once. What's our rendezvous track with the Hukk force look like?"

"We'll intercept almost at the Lunar surface; maybe ten thousand miles out, depending on the deceleration elements used—"

"Emergency max. I want them inside the Terran cone of shadow, but just barely."

Darcy nodded. "If they're what you think—and I've got a nasty feeling they are—they've got us outnumbered and outgunned five to one. What happens when we meet 'em?"

"I'll let you know when the time comes," Dalton said.

CHAPTER FOUR

It was almost nine hours before the signals major was able to report a confirmed ID on the unknown ninety-nine heavy Hukk fireships.

"That's the biggest damned Hukk fleet ever fielded," Darcy said in tones of awe. "They must have been saving up for this punch for years!"

"I'm picking up another incoming alert beam from supreme HQ via Luna relay," the signals officer announced.

"Same instructions, no response," Dalton ordered.

"Tan—that's SHQ calling—as sure as our court-martials—"

"Courts-martial," Dalton corrected. "Or court-martial: *you're* covered. It's *my* neck. Just follow your orders."

Darcy looked uncomfortable. "Sure—but—"

"If I acknowledge, the Hukk will intercept my transmission. They might even tap the outbound if they have a picket out on the flank for the purpose—"

There was a sharp tone from a warning screen. Both men turned alertly to it.

"I have an incoming spy trace," the signals officer reported tensely. "Nine plus ID as a Hukk LR probe. Seems to be a new type—" He broke off. "That's it," he said. "I have their beam now; it's tightening up. A definite contact, they've got us pinpointed." The man turned to stare up worriedly at the ranking officers.

"All right, you can AK Luna's beam now," Dalton said. "The cat's out of the bag."

There was a brief chatter of equipment.

"It's a PC, sir—for your information only," the communications officer announced.

"Pipe it to channel three." Dalton switched on his ear set, adjusted the throat mike.

"Dalton reporting," he subvocalized.

"Dalton!" It was the excited voice of Undersecretary Treech. "What the devil's going on out there! You were instructed to keep me informed on a continuing basis! I haven't had a report from you since you lifted—and now I'm advised that you've aborted rendezvous and are on an emergency course for base! What's happened? What—"

"Communications difficulties, Mr. Undersecretary," Dalton cut into the excited outburst, which continued unabated for another half-minute.

". . . want a complete report, you understand? Why've you failed to AK my tracer? Why—" The Undersecretary broke off as Dalton's first words reached him, resumed almost at once:

"Bah! What kind of communications difficulties? Any one of the twenty-seven vessels under your command have baseline capability! What kind of smoke screen is this, Dalton? Did you get cold feet at the last minute? I suppose this means Veidt's assumed command by now and is preparing to plunge us into full-scale war!"

"I relieved Admiral Starbird at oh-nine/three-one/six-two hours, IAW Departmental ESO 54," Dalton said. "Further communications negative at this time. Dalton out."

"That was short," Darcy said. "Ah—what—?"

"I told them I couldn't talk," Dalton said.

"My God, Tan—aren't you going to tell them?"

"Not necessary," Dalton said. His eyes were on the triagram, where the Hukk fleet continued steadily on course in tight formation.

"What are we going to do?" Darcy asked.

"I want them a little closer," Dalton said. "Then we'll see how good that task force commander is at thinking on his feet."

"You can't be planning to just chew into them, Tan; we'd never stand a chance!"

"Uh-uh, this won't be a fire test, George. We're going to take them the easy way."

"Another Luna relay alert," the communications officer announced. "Shall I put it on three, sir?"

"Negative. Continue comm silence."

"They know we're here," Darcy said, still watching the triagram. "But they don't give a damn. They haven't varied course a millimeter; still bunched up, bee-lining it for target. Luna'll spot them any time now."

"Don't count on it. Luna depends on Terra relay for LR detection. And they're not anticipating a goblin formation in the inner range. What's Hunneker doing?"

"Still hanging on the fringe. Think they've plotted him yet?"

"Let's give them some help," Dalton said. "Give him a one-millisec squirt on the tightest line you can squeeze out of your equipment."

"Yessir. What intelligence?"

"Nothing. Just an unmodulated squawk."

"All that'll do is tip the Hukk off he's out there—if they don't already know."

"It'll add to the air of mystery."

"You're operating way over my head, Commodore."

"They'll be wondering now; but if they'll hold their present course and disposition for another half-hour or so, we'll have 'em."

"Well—they'll hold course as long as they can, I guess—they can't stray far off line without losing Luna as a shield—but what good will that do us? They've faked us out of position—"

"So maybe two can play at the game."

"Would you want to spell that out any further, Tan?"

"They decoyed us out to Piranha with a phony concentration. What if we'd been shrewd enough to take 'em up on it—with a fake fleet of our own?"

"Sure—but we didn't."

"They don't know that."

"So—if we're not out at Piranha waiting for the laugh—where *are* we?"

"Well, part of us *could* be here . . ." Dalton used a light-pointer to indicate a position high above the ecliptic, on the far side of Luna. ". . . and part of us could be over here." He indicated a second position symmetrically placed with regard to the Hukk task force.

"Doing what?"

"Coming in at full gate on converging course lines."

"Mmm. In another half-hour they'd be in Hukk detector range—if they were there. But by then they'd be obscured behind Luna."

"I'll give them that half-hour," Dalton said. "Then

punch a beam through to the Hukk force commander and give him the bad news."

"You think he'll believe it?"

"Why shouldn't he? It's simple enough. His fleet's bunched; a three-way fleet-force strike will wipe him out of space like shooting alligators in the bathtub."

"Tan—you mean it's true? Starbird met the Hukk with a decoy?" Darcy grinned suddenly. "Oh, brother, are Veidt and Borgman going to love sitting on the sidelines while *we* handle the action!"

"That's the spirit, George."

A murmur of conversation had gone around the command deck as the word was passed that the main Terran fleet was approaching to close the jaws of a three-way trap. Darcy was in a keen mood now, smiling and alert. Dalton watched the vectors in the tank. The gap between the Terran forward elements and the giant Hukk force gradually diminished as both plunged toward Luna, vast on the screens now, twenty thousand miles away. The gap closed. . . .

"That's it!" Dalton said at last. "Raise the Hukk commander for me."

Another minute passed in tense silence. The TMX screen lit up, flickered for a moment, steadied into a view of the communications deck of a Hukk ship of the line. The Hukk officer on duty there stared out of the screen, his alien features as complicated and unreadable as those of a crab. There was a brief exchange between him and Dalton in the dialect known as Hukk 9; then the scene shifted. A larger-than-average Hukk with a string of rank discs on his sloping shoulders turned to gaze out at the Terrans. The cluster of digital members beside his slablike cheeks twitched restlessly.

"I am Second Admiral H'noorn," he said in nasal but clearly enunciated Terran. "Hwhat is it hyou hwish?" He spoke as calmly as if the encounter were a matter of routine.

"I'm Commodore Dalton, Terran Space Arm. Kindly put your first admiral on screen."

There was a ten-second lag.

"Fhor hwat purpose?"

"I'm calling on him for immediate unconditional surrender," Dalton said flatly.

Again the pregnant silence while the signal crossed space, was unscrambled and translated.

"Indheed? May I phoint out that it hwas nhot for this purpose that the first admiral bhrought the Grand Armada here."

"Nevertheless, I suggest you put him on—unless you're ready to accept full responsibility."

"Hwait." H'noorn turned away and spoke rapidly in what Dalton thought was Hukk 12, a technical dialect of which he knew only a few words. He caught "extraordinary" and "discretion." The screen winked, and a different Hukk officer was there.

"Saanch'k, First Admiral," he said in a hollow tone. "I am advhised you have invited me to htender the capitulation of hmy command. Hmy curiosity is aroused."

Dalton's eyes flicked to the master plot chronometer. "You have fifteen minutes and thirty seconds in which to signal your intention to yield your force, or I shall commit full force to the attack."

"Indheed? Am I to understand that hyour small detachment mounts weaponry of a totally new order of effectiveness, without which it can obviously present no threat to me?"

"Negative, Admiral."

"Hso. I appreciate hyour candor, Commodore. However, I hmust of course decline to accept hyour invitation—"

"Time's passing, Admiral. They didn't send you out here to lose a fleet. You've been outmaneuvered. Your position is hopeless. Capitulate at once, before any unfortunate incident occurs that will make it impossible for our two governments to regard this exercise as an innocent miscalculation on your part."

"An interestingh proposal, Commodore. Khindly show me in hwat light my position could be regarded as hopeless, as hyou put it."

"Admiral, if you'll have the following vectors plotted into your situation tank . . ." He read off two sets of figures. "You'll see that fleets at those loci could cross course behind Luna in twelve minutes and emerge from Luna shadow precisely twenty-one minutes later in such positions on both your exposed flanks as to interdict any attempted escape maneuver by your tightly grouped forces. By such forces, together with my own force, you will be effectively englobed, and occupying the point of focus of the massed firepower of the entire Terran Home Fleet."

Saanch'k turned jerkily away, speaking rapidly:

". . . enfilade . . . backplot . . . undetectible . . . ," Dalton caught.

The Hukk admiral was back. "Your hmain fleet is hknown to be at this time on station for fleet hrendezvous hmaneuvers in the hvicinity of the Piranha System," he said rapidly.

"In order to confront your own Grand Armada, eh?" Dalton smiled a consciously grim smile. "I think we're both aware of the capabilities of modern electronic decoys, Admiral."

Saanch'k stared unreadably out at Dalton. "Hyou ask hme to belicve that hyour fleet has hnot in fact proceeded to the station announced by your own hnews service—"

"The same news service, I believe, which has been

reporting the assembly of a Hukk force in the same vicinity for some months now, Admiral." Dalton's tone changed. "I suggest we stop wasting time, sir. Unless a countermand order is issued—by me—every vessel that emerges from Lunar shadow twenty-one minutes from now will open fire without further orders. You can save your fleet, if not your face. Decide quickly."

Saanch'k turned from the screen again to confer excitedly with half a dozen Hukk officers. He turned back to Dalton.

"Commodore, under orders of hmy High Command, I have, during the past three standard hmonths, assembled the largest, hmost hmodern, best equipped fleet ever fielded by the Hukk Empire—"

"The Dongen's Cluster's no secret, Admiral," Dalton interrupted callously.

"Hso." Saanch'k's digits twitched restlessly. "I am now proceeding hwith that force, in accordance with commands issued under the personal cartouche of the High Emperor, to carry out the hreduction and investment of an objective hnow less than two hours standard distant. Hnow, suddenly, hyou appear—accompanied by a force of less than a third the hweight of hmine—and suggest that the Hukk Grand Strategy is bankrupt, that I have been deluded, that hmassive Terran forces even hnow approach for hmy destruction—"

"Very well summarized, Admiral. Nine minutes. You'll signal your capitulation by ordering every unit of your command to shut down all power, and assume docking orientation in pairs, stern-to-stern, the maneuver to be accomplished before the expiration of the deadline."

"How do hyou propose to confirm hyour contention that forces capable of overwhelming the Grand Armada are approaching under cover of Luna?"

"I don't."

"Hyou demand hmy surrender of a vastly hmore powerful force to hyour tiny command, on the basis of an unsupported statement?"

"Admiral, I could have let you proceed unsuspecting. Having warned you, I have no further responsibility. The decision is yours. Eight minutes."

Saanch'k stared out at Dalton, unmoving for a full ten seconds.

"This could be hno hmore than an audacious bluff, Commodore. If I refuse—and if hyou persist on hyour present overhaul course—and if at the end of eight hminutes—"

"Seven and a half."

"—hyour fleet fails to appear—hyour position hwill be impossible."

"Seven minutes."

"If I *should* consider an alteration of course in order to ahvoid an unfortunate hmisunderstanding—" Saanch'k said quickly.

"Negative. Shut down main power and assume docking orientation as ordered or suffer the consequences."

"Commodore—if hyou're lying—and I hknow that hyou Terrans are quite capable of it—"

"Five and one half minutes," Dalton said calmly.

The Hukk admiral stared at Dalton for a moment longer; then the screen blanked.

"What do you think, Tan?" Darcy said tightly. "Will he fold? Or will we have to blow 'em out of space?"

"We'll know soon," Dalton snapped. Darcy glanced sideways at his superior's tense features, intent on the situation tank. For half a minute the blinking yellow blip representing the Hukk force continued on course. Then, abruptly, it went to a steady glow.

"They've shut down main power!" someone said loudly.

"By God," Darcy said, sounding almost regretful. "I half-expected him to tell us to go to hell and then scatter with all guns blazing. But that wouldn't be Hukk style, I suppose. They like to bet on sure things."

"Sir, units of Hukk force maneuvering on secondary power," a monitor reported. "Assuming docking configuration."

"Hold the screen open for Saanch'k," Dalton said curtly. Another minute passed. The flotilla was within a thousand miles of the Hukk force now—practically point-blank range. "Keep all tubes aligned on designated targets," Dalton said.

"Hell, Tan, you don't think they'll try a double-cross *now?*" Darcy protested. "Not in docking orientation; they can't use main power without killing each other—"

The Hukk admiral reappeared. "In the interest of the avhoidance of an unfortunate incident," he said in his rather metallic voice, "and as evidence of good-hwill, I have acceded to hyour hrequest, Commodore Dalton. I propose to take no further action until the hremainder of hyour force has put in an appearance—"

"Negative," Dalton said curtly. "You'll proceed at once to disarm all weapons-control circuitry. I'll monitor your compliance via your master indicator panels. Kindly have a pickup focused there at once."

"Outrageous! I—"

"Four minutes," Dalton cut in flatly.

"Vhery hwell! But hyou hmay be sure that this hmatter hwill be brought to the attention of hmy government at the highest level!"

"It certainly will. I suggest you hurry, Admiral. My orders allow for no time extensions."

Dalton watched as commands were given; on the master board on the command deck of the alien craft, bank after bank of ready lights died. In less than two minutes the enemy fire-control systems were inert.

"If he's kidding us," Darcy muttered, "cutting indicator lights intead of pulling his actual fire control—"

"Hvery hwell, Commodore," the Hukk admiral reported. "I have demonstrated the earnest desire of the Hukk government to avoid any hmisunderstanding hwhich might lead to unfortunate consequences. I trust hyou are satisfied?"

"You'll now alter course to enter Lunar orbit at an altitude of one thousand miles standard," Dalton ordered. "Any evidence of use of primary power for purposes unconnected with this authorized course change will be interpreted as a hostile act and will be dealt with accordingly."

"For hwat purpose—?" Saanch'k started, but Dalton cut him off.

"No queries, Admiral. Execute!"

On the screens, the Hukk vessels edged apart, turned, blasted briefly, their drives glaring a characteristic vivid pink, taking up their new paths.

"Neat," Darcy commented. "Those boys are fast learners. I couldn't have cut that prettier myself."

The Hukk admiral reappeared. "I trust hyou are nhow satisfied, Commodore? Hwith hyour permission, I hwill hnow communicate hwith hmy government's Embassy at Hwashington—"

"Negative," Dalton said flatly. "You'll come aboard my flagship now to sign the articles of capitulation."

The Hukk's facial appendages writhed. "Outrageous! By all the hrules of intergovernmental concourse—"

"I'm making the rules for now, Admiral. You'll report aboard my flagship—"

"Nhever! This hwould constitute an insupportable affront to the hmajesty of the High Emperor, hwhose personal emissary I have the honor to be!"

"I have no wish to offer any insult to his High Majesty," Dalton said formally, "but your immediate presence aboard my ship is mandatory."

Again Saanch'k blanked his screen.

"Maybe you ought to settle for well enough," Darcy suggested diffidently. "The Hukk are funny critters; he just might balk now, which would leave us with the option of backing down or blasting hell out of a helpless target."

"He'll figure out an answer."

"You're pushing the old boy to the wall," Darcy said. "Why risk the whole thing for a few protocol points?"

"The protocols don't mean much to us," Dalton said, "but they're big medicine to the Hukk. I don't want any question later about who capitulated to whom."

Saanch'k reappeared.

"I have hreached a decision, Commodore," he stated. "I hwill be happy to hvisit hyou aboard your flagship—provided an officer of appropriate hrank first hreports to hme in the capacity of escort."

Dalton hesitated for only a moment. "Very well," he said. "An escort will be designated."

"I hmust inquire the hname and hrank of the designated officer," Saanch'k said in a tone hwhich rang hwith finality.

"Commodore Tancredi Dalton, FSA, acting admiral," Dalton said promptly.

"Hey—" Darcy started, and fell silent.

"I hmust point out," Saanch'k said harshly, "that

the hrank of commodore is hardly commensurate hwith hmy own—"

"I'm sure that you will not wish to offer any gratuitous offense to me as acting admiral by rejection of myself as escort," Dalton cut in roughly.

"I . . . find hyour designation acceptable," Saanch'k said somewhat reluctantly. "Kindly hmatch course hwith hme."

"Negative. You'll carry out the maneuvering."

"As hyou hwish," Saanch'k said stiffly, and switched off.

"The old devil's up to something," Darcy said tightly. "Don't fall for it. I'll go across. I'm a line captain—that ought to be rank enough for them."

"No. I'm going."

Darcy looked at him. "It doesn't make sense—from a purely tactical viewpoint. With you as hostage, he's got leverage. Why give him even the possibility of that advantage?"

"We're in command of the situation, George. This isn't the time to start getting cautious. If I refused now he might start thinking some of the things I don't want him to think. I'm not taking that chance."

On the screens a single Hukk vessel separated itself from the main body, drifted closer to the Terran formation.

"I have him on the fine screen, sir," a technician called.

"Initiate matching maneuver," Darcy ordered. Minutes passed; the only sounds on the deck were the terse exchanges among the duty officers. There was a brief rumble of secondary power, the slight vertigo of reorientation, the faint tug of acceleration, then of braking.

Second Admiral H'noorn appeared on the screen.

"The first admiral is prepared to receive hyou

aboard, Commodore," he said. "You hwill of course be unaccompanied."

"Like hell," Darcy said, but subsided at a curt gesture from Dalton.

"Of course," he said.

"I hneed hardly hmention that the hwearing of side-arms hwould be regarded as an affront to the integrity of a hvessel bearing the Emperor's commission," H'noorn added.

"My orders don't require me to wear a sidearm in this situation," Dalton said evenly. "I therefore do not intend to wear one."

"Hyou hmay come aboard hnow," the second admiral stated curtly.

"I'll advise you when I'm prepared to board," Dalton said, and cut the connection.

"I don't like this," Darcy said quickly. "Not even a little. Why *you*, Tan, alone and unarmed?"

"We can afford to let them have the points. And they could lock up a party of ten as easily as one. By going alone I demonstrate my dominance of the situation. They wouldn't put it quite that way, of course, but they'll get the message."

"I'll be watching," Darcy said grimly. "One false move out of them, and they won't know what hit them."

"Negative, George. If anything goes wrong from this point on, you'll disperse the flotilla at full emergency blast and beam a full-scale Mayday to every station on the primary list."

"Disperse?" Darcy echoed. "That sounds like—"

"Never mind what it sounds like. See that it happens."

2

Dalton descended to the hatch deck, suited up, entered the lock. Air cycled. The outer port opened, and a puff of frosty air expelled him into space.

Luna dominated the sky, a dazzling silver-white crescent as big as a man's palm held at arm's length. The Hukk vessels were points of brilliant reflection, ranked in an open array that stretched off to be lost in the moon's glare. Far to the left, a single Terran vessel was a tiny cluster of lights. The Hukk flagship loomed above, half a mile distant, a gigantic and baroque shape, dark against the stars but for paired lights at bow and stern and the amber glow of the open port.

The crossing was uneventful. A pair of black-and-yellow-uniformed Hukk sailors met Dalton at the port, saluted, and assisted him to unsuit. The Hukk air was chilly and smelled of cucumbers, but was breathable.

Saanch'k met him in the navigation room: neutral territory, Dalton deduced, neither the cold informality of the commander's lounge nor the implied cordiality of the bridge. The Hukk first admiral wore gray—the formal color among his kind—and carried a heavy brass-colored ring that Dalton knew was solid gold, a badge of office, clutched in one of the bony members that served him as arms. The two leaders exchanged formal greetings. Together they descended to the loading deck. Dalton resumed his suit, and they mounted a small, powered platform, which maneuvered carefully through the open hatch.

The return crossing was equally without incident. Aboard the Terran destroyer, Saanch'k seemed subdued, almost uninterested. At Dalton's order a lengthy document had been produced, setting forth the terms of the Hukk surrender. Saanch'k glanced at it and struck it with his secondary fist, impressing the Hukk equivalent of a fingerprint on the thin plastic sheet. Dalton appended his signature.

"If this completes the formalities," Saanch'k said, "I hwill nhow return to hmy command."

"On the contrary, Admiral, you'll be my guest for a while."

"Nhothing hwas said of this."

"Nevertheless, I must insist."

"For hwhat purpose do hyou propose to hold hme here—and for how hlong?"

"Until I have covering instructions from higher command."

"Ah—a hmatter of a few hmoments, then—until the arrival of the other elements of hyour force." The Hukk admiral turned to gaze at the chronometer. "Some five hminutes, by hyour reckoning; about two and a third *charr*."

"It might take a little longer," Dalton said. "Captain Darcy, kindly raise Fleet SHQ, and please find comfortable quarters for Admiral Saanch'k."

"Certainly." Darcy gave orders to an officer, who escorted the Hukk admiral away. Darcy turned back to Dalton. "Would you like me to request Lunar Relay to stand by to pass a signal to the fleet?"

"That won't be necessary."

Darcy looked blank. "I don't understand. If they're scheduled to emerge from behind Luna in a couple of minutes—"

"Don't wait up for them."

"—and we haven't notified them, they'll start blasting as soon as . . ." Darcy's voice died away; then he resumed:

"Tan—surely—after taking their surrender, you're not going to stand by and let the attack go forward!"

"There'll be no attack."

"But—"

"I know. I guess I gave you a false impression."

Darcy paled visibly. "You mean—no fleet? We tackled the Grand Armada with our bare hands?"

"Our bare mouths," Dalton corrected.

"He walked right in here—meek as a lamb! Their fighting admiral! Tan—how did you know—how could you be so cocksure fire-eating Admiral Saanch'k would fold?"

"He's playing the game, too, George. He was sent out here to make some easy points for his side, not to lose a fleet—or to take even the ghost of a chance of losing it."

"He handed it over," Darcy cried wondrously, "like a kid turning in his cap pistol to the principal! To *us!* With nothing! For God's sake, Tan—when Saanch'k finds out—!"

"Sir—I have an incoming Fleet Urgent, via Luna seven," a technician called.

"Put him on," Dalton said. The screen winked alight, showing the excited face of a duty officer. Dalton requested a conference with the commander of Terra Base One. Half a minute later the stern visage of Vice Admiral French appeared.

"Dalton, what's this all about?" he demanded. "I have a report from Admiral Starbird that you've taken the unprecedented step of advising your superior officer that he was relieved of duty, citing some sort of imaginary Departmental Special Order. Not only him, but his chief of staff, and his senior fleet commander."

"That's correct, sir—except that the DSO wasn't imaginary—"

"You admit it? Don't you realize what you're confessing, Dalton? This is mutiny in Deep Space—in the face of the enemy—"

"Correction, sir. Not mutiny—and not in the face of the enemy. There were no Hukk out at Piranha, just a couple of joke wagons. I—"

"Dalton, are you out of your mind? Where are you? I understand your incoming signal was passed on here by Lunar Relay—"

"I'm in Lunar orbit, sir. I wish to report—"

"You admit you've actually taken your flotilla out of action—violated direct orders—run like a whipped cur for home—"

"Sir, I have an urgent report. I'm holding First Admiral Saanch'k in custody aboard my flagship. The Hukk Grand Armada is disarmed and in docking formation, holding Lunar orbit. I'm awaiting further instructions."

"The Hukk *what?* Dalton—you're insane! Put Captain Darcy on screen at once!"

Darcy stepped up and reported snappily.

"Darcy, Commodore Dalton's suffered a breakdown, quite apparently," French stated harshly. "Place him under close confinement at once. You'll consider yourself in temporary command of the flotilla until relief arrives, understood?"

"Yes, sir," Darcy said briskly. "Just one question, sir: what do I do with the Hukk admiral and the Hukk fleet in the meantime?"

CHAPTER FIVE

It was almost two hours—time enough for Dalton and the captive fleet to complete a Lunar transit in full view of Terrestrial observers—before Admiral French again contacted Dalton.

"I don't pretend to understand all this, Dalton," he said gruffly. "Apparently there were schemes afoot of which even I was not fully informed. Plans formulated by the Council, that is to say," he amended, recalling that his words were being recorded. "Which presumably were restricted to personnel actually involved. I can't say I fully approve in principle of such operations"—he caught himself again—"but of course as a military man, I take orders, as we all do. I'm reconfirming you in your temporary command, pending complete investigation, of course. I'm, ah, issuing orders retroactive to oh-seven plus thirty hours detaching your unit and directing you to intercept and take captive the Hukk intruders. The orders will be issued over the signatures of Admiral Starbird and Admiral

Veidt. I see no point in making issue at this time of any, ah, lack of complete coordination of the planned action . between you and your superiors. Reinforcements are now en route from Piranha. You'll turn local command over to Admiral Borgman on his arrival, and receive further instructions direct from him."

"Funny business," Darcy said after the senior admiral had switched off, "transmitting your orders via Borgman. Why not pass them direct? I wonder what's up?"

"I assume we'll find out in six hours," Dalton said. "Meantime, I need some sleep."

2

The courier vessel bearing Borgman arrived on schedule, docked with Dalton's flagship, still in Lunar orbit astern the silent Hukk formation. The admiral came aboard, greeted Dalton curtly.

"I'll speak to you privately, Dalton," he said. "We'll go to your quarters."

"I suggest we talk here, Admiral. I don't want to leave the bridge at this time."

"This is for your ears only," Borgman said curtly. "Let's go."

Dalton turned to Darcy. "George, please rig a hush-phone for the admiral."

Borgman grunted but acceded without further demur. The closed-link set was plugged in at his elbow, keyed to Dalton's set.

"Never liked these damn things," Borgman said. "Feel like a fool sitting here whispering. However . . ." He gave Dalton an assessing look. "I'll get right to the point, Dalton. There were a number of us who didn't know where you stood. I see now you're in the confidence of the right people. That was a rather unsettling way of handling this affair—springing it on all of us as you did—but I assume there were adequate reasons for keeping the rest of us in the dark. I'll have to revise my opinion of FSA HQ grand strategy: after all, it's results that count." Borgman's features registered a savage satisfaction.

"The main fleet will arrive in less than one hour," he went on. "They'll deploy in standard formation alpha nine green. You'll retain your present formation until zero minus thirty; then you'll take position as third element of the overall configuration."

"H'noorn will be monitoring your approach," Dalton pointed out. "It might upset him to see the fleet coming in in an attack formation."

"Let it; it'll be too late then for him to do anything about it."

"If he panics, there could be some nasty incidents: loss of life, even—"

Borgman flashed an intent look at Dalton. "Not on *our* side," he said tightly. "We've got the bastards where we want them."

"Maybe you'd better spell that out a little plainer, Admiral," Dalton said expressionlessly.

"How plain do you want it? It's obvious, isn't it? We've maneuvered the damned pirates into an ambush. They came poking into Home Space. Fine. We'll show them what that buys them."

"Just what *does* it buy them?"

Borgman doubled a fist and slammed it into his palm. "Annihilation!" he said. "We'll blow their damned fleet out of space! And then we'll go back and clean out the nest on their home planet and then go on to burn out the infected spots at Doon 8 and Auclaire IV and V. We'll make a clean sweep of it."

"I accepted Saanch'k's surrender," Dalton said mildly.

"That was as good a way as any of stalling him until the main force could come up," Borgman said absently. "As I see it, we could effect a fifty percent disabling rate with the first salvo; that's assuming that last-minute evasive maneuvers are attempted at, say, zero minus fifteen. Far too late to do them any good. Thereafter it'll be open-formation independent actions. For this phase, I've designated a buddy system, each unit pairing with a complementary vessel for a two-to-one ratio, for the cleanup. My most conservative estimate indicates that we'll effect a ninety-eight-plus percentage kill. Hukk space power will be permanently broken. The mopping up of their outstations and colonies and investing of the home planet will be a mere routine fleet exercise." Borgman looked sharply at Dalton.

"I'll have to hand it to you, Dalton: you handled your end very effectively. You do as well in the coming action, and I'll personally see to it that High Command knows about it."

"Maybe you didn't hear me, Admiral," Dalton said quietly. "I said I accepted the surrender of the Hukk armada."

"What's that?" Borgman said impatiently. "Of course I heard you. What—"

"I signed articles guaranteeing the Hukk the integrity of their vessels," Dalton continued.

"Integrity, hell! The murdering back-stabbers—"

". . . and granting self-police authority and safe conduct to all crewmen," Dalton added.

"What the hell are you asking me to do?" Borgman barked. "Take off the personnel before we blow their ships out of space? Utterly impractical! At the first hint of what we intend, they'd open fire. Their position would be hopeless, of course, but we'd suffer needless casualties. Negative, Dalton. This isn't the time for half-baked humanitarian gestures."

"I wasn't thinking of taking off the crews, Admiral."

"Out of the question," Borgman grumped. "How the devil would we house and feed that horde of crabheads? No point in it—"

"Maybe I'm not getting through," Dalton said calmly. "Under the terms of the surrender our action will be limited to stripping the Hukk vessels of their offensive capability, after which they'll be free to proceed home."

Borgman stared at Dalton. "So? Tell 'em whatever you have to to get them where you want them—fine. What about it?"

"The Hukk can't afford to lose a hundred space hulls," Dalton said. "It would set their economy back fifty years. That's how long it's taken to assemble and outfit this fleet—"

"What in the name of the Nine Hells do I care how far back it sets the goddamned crabs?" Borgman roared, loudly enough that every head in the room turned to gape.

"Look here, Dalton," he went on in a lower tone, taut with anger, "I thought I'd misjudged you: you went in there like a Navy man ought to and stopped these devils in their tracks—showed them who the hell they were dealing with—that poking their damned snouts into Home Space was bad news for Hukks with big ideas. Now you're spouting Softline mush at me! Where the hell do you stand, man!"

"I'm standing on my agreement with Saanch'k,"

"The hell you say! You're a fool, Dalton—a softheaded fool! You had me fooled. All you had to do was sit quietly and carry out your orders and you'd have weathered this thing without a black mark in your record. Instead, you give me this *crap!* This Softline propaganda, this sob-sister line about the poor, deserving Hukk!"

"I don't remember using any of those terms. I said I'd given my word—"

"Your word," Borgman said in a deadly tone, "is going to be in the same boat with Dr. Mudd's, if I hear any more of this insubordinate hogwash out of you. I never liked you, Dalton; I'll tell you plainly. I was willing to forget all that on the basis of what you accomplished here. Well, you've blown that! You've shown me a glimpse of the Softline rot inside you, and I'm not the man to forget that." Borgman sat up straight and exhaled through his nostrils.

"Now, Dalton, if you want to hold on to your command here, you'll get your head right and carry out your orders with all the vigor I expect of a loyal subordinate!"

"Negative, Admiral," Dalton said.

Borgman's eyes narrowed. "What did you say?" he asked quietly.

"I haven't received any orders, Admiral. Any legal ones, I mean."

Borgman's face went taut. "All right—if you want to nit-pick, Dalton. Here are your orders: You'll relinquish command of the flotilla to me as of now and report yourself under arrest in quarters. Is that clear?"

"Clear," Dalton said crisply. "But meaningless."

"By God, the meaning's clear enough. Darcy!" Borgman ripped away the hushphone and yelled the last word. The young captain stepped to his side.

"I'm assuming direct command of the flotilla," Borgman snapped. "Dalton's relieved. You'll continue in command here."

Darcy, standing at attention, said nothing.

"Is that clear?" Borgman barked.

"No, sir," Darcy said.

"What the hell do you mean 'no'!"

"He means you can't relieve me, Admiral," Dalton said. "I'm in temporary supreme command, as you'll no doubt recall. You're under *my* orders, not the reverse."

"Don't try that one on *me,*" Borgman yelled. "Maybe Starbird and Veidt were timid enough to sit still for it, but—"

"So did you," Dalton said, "and quite rightly. My orders are still in effect—"

"Negative—even if those hoked-up so-called orders ever existed, which I doubt—Admiral French has since countermanded them, putting you back under my direct command, and you damned well know it!"

"A vice admiral can't overrule a Departmental SO," Dalton said.

"A space lawyer, eh! You know damned well what the intent was—"

"For the present, I'm retaining command," Dalton said flatly.

"Oh?" Borgman glared from Dalton to Darcy. "Are you in this with him, Darcy?"

"Sir, I have no choice but to obey a legal command."

"Like that, eh?" Borgman whirled on Dalton. "All right—you missed one bet, Dalton. It occurred to some of us that you might pull something—some obstructionist tactic—but I admit not even I expected barefaced mutiny. Accordingly, Admiral Veidt is under orders, if on his approach he finds you not in position to support his attack, to proceed without you—and without further confirmation from me! So you can do your damnedest! And hang for it!"

"Maybe you'd better get on the horn and countermand that, Admiral," Dalton said. "If the fleet approaches in attack formation, I'll have no choice but to open fire."

"You'd fire on your own kind?" Borgman said in a tone of utter incredulity. He shook his gray head. "You've gone mad," he said. "If you did—if you so far forgot every decent principle of loyalty and duty as to fire on your own shipmates—you'd be blasted out of space! The Blue and Orange fleets outnumber your flotilla over two to one!"

"True. But I won't be alone, of course."

"What the hell does that mean?" Borgman growled.

"I'll have the Hukk Grand Armada to back me up," Dalton said.

3

"You'd really have done it, wouldn't you, Dalton?" Borgman said dully, half an hour later, after orders had gone out to the Blue and Orange fleets to modify course and stand by for escort duty. "You'd have rearmed those alien devils and led them into battle against your own comrades."

"It was all academic," Dalton said. "Since it didn't come to that."

"Pretty proud of yourself, aren't you, Dalton?" the admiral said. "Leading us all by the noses, running your bluffs. But your hour's about to end—"

"Incoming fleet urgent," the signals lieutenant called. At Dalton's order, he put the call on screen.

"Dalton—a fine piece of work," Undersecretary Treech said heartily. "I confess I was at sixes and sevens there for a bit, when I learned that you'd made use of the Special Order I'd given you to overrule Borgman and Veidt, and thereupon pulled your flotilla out of line and streaked for home. I'll have something to say to you about that later, but in view of the outcome—" he broke off as he caught sight of Borgman standing by, a grim expression on his weathered face.

"Well, Admiral," he said, and paused, frowning. "Inasmuch as you're on the scene, it might be a good idea for you to take over liaison with our, ah, guests—"

"Guests!" Borgman spat out the word like a bite of wormy apple.

"I'll remind you, Borgman," Treech said sharply, "that thanks to Commodore Dalton's carefully restrained actions, a very nasty incident has been avoided. Officially, nothing has occurred but a simple violation of Terran space—a mere misunderstanding—"

"I understand well enough, Mr. Undersecretary! Too damn well!"

"That will be enough, Admiral!" Treech snapped. "Commodore Dalton's presence is required in Washington immediately. His report, as you'll understand, is of the utmost interest not only to the Department but to the Council as well." The Undersecretary's glance went back to Dalton.

"I suspect you'll be lionized to a degree, Commodore: the rumor seems to have spread that you single-handedly saved the planet from destruction. Even those of us on the inside are aware that we owe you a debt of gratitude. What a hothead might have done in your situation— But never mind that sort of speculation. You may consider this as your official orders to report to FSA HQ with all dispatch. The crews who'll carry out the, ah, modifications to the Hukk vessels will be arriving shortly; I suggest you come back down with one of the shuttles. Admiral Borgman, you'll carry on. You know the details."

"I know." Borgman grunted. "Pat 'em on the head and send 'em home," he added in a mutter.

"And I don't need to remind you," Treech said sharply, "that any deviation whatever from your instructions will be viewed in the gravest light by this department." He looked flatly at the admiral.

"There'll be no incident," Borgman said. "I know how to carry out orders—even if I don't particularly like 'em."

After the Undersecretary signed off, Dalton formally turned over command to the older man.

"What passed between us here isn't in the record," Dalton said. "I don't intend to mention it. As far as I'm concerned, it was all conversation."

"Covering your tracks already, eh, Dalton?" Borgman stared at him balefully. "Smart of you—not that you could prove anything, since you wiped the record. For the moment you're Treech's fair-haired boy—that treacherous Softlining swine! You've managed your damned double-crossing piece of duplicity very cleverly. But political winds change fast. You'll find your patron Treech fading into the wallpaper as soon as the real story of this act of treason leaks out—as it will, I'll see to that. The world will learn that their hero had the enemy under his guns and let him go. And when the time comes, Dalton—well, I have a long memory. I don't like insubordinate upstarts. And what I don't like I destroy." He turned on his heel and stalked away.

CHAPTER SIX

"I confess I didn't like it at all at first, Dalton," Senator Kelvin said, running his fingers through his white hair. "When word was flashed to me that you'd ignored my suggestion to clean out Petreac and Leadpipe and instead had relieved Starbird—and headed home, I frankly thought you'd sold out to Treech and his pack. Then the news arrived that you'd stolen a march on the enemy and had them penned up like sheep ready for the slaughter, and I revised my opinion. I saw the opportunity to end this situation once and for all—a Final Solution." Kelvin closed his fist as if he were cracking nuts.

"Damn it, it was a brilliant coup, Dalton! I couldn't believe it when I heard that you'd defied French's orders and turned them loose."

"Luckily, those orders were never committed to my log, Senator," Dalton said.

"I know, I know," Kelvin said testily. "And of

course the opportunity was lost forever when that Softlining traitor Treech confirmed your action—made it official. Not that I'm tarring you with the same brush. Not precisely. You played into his hands—but innocently, I'm willing to assume."

Dalton said nothing. Kelvin sighed and shook his head. "And now, of course, it's apparent that the backlash from what the yellow press would have called a massacre might have been more than we'd bargained for." The senator shot Dalton an almost furtive look. "So I suppose I should be grateful, in the final analysis. In my zeal to end this Hukk menace, perhaps I was prepared to go too far. Perhaps you saved me—and others—from a tactical blunder." Kelvin's expression hardened. "I'm willing to concede that—privately. But my colleagues are not so minded. They feel you sold them out, Dalton. Under the circumstances, any, ah, commitments I may have seemed to have made earlier must of course be considered as abrogated. I'm sure you understand."

"I'm sure I do," Dalton said. "Is that all, Senator?"

"One other thing," Kelvin said. "It might be best if you saw no more of Arianne for a time. There are those who might place a false interpretation on it. And at this point—with the Softliners riding high—thanks to you—I can't afford even a hint that would weaken my support base among my colleagues."

"That seems to cover everything, Senator," Dalton said.

"I hope so, Dalton." Kelvin gazed at him assessingly. "You had an opportunity, out there, to play a role in great affairs. The way you handled it . . . I don't know, Dalton. I don't know."

"Goodbye, Senator. Thanks for the drink."

2

"What did he say, darling?"

"He told me I'd blown my big chance to run interference for the Hardliners."

"Don't be bitter, Tan."

"I hope I don't sound bitter."

"You don't—but . . . maybe *I* would be. Damn! You saved their bacon—even if it did make Treech and his friends dance a jig in their big plush-lined offices—"

"No plusher than a senior senator's."

"Daddy's a sincere man, Tan. You have to believe that. Even if—"

"Even if his convictions sometimes force him into difficult positions."

"Yes—exactly. He believes the Hukk are a mortal threat to the human race; that they'll push and push until they end by overwhelming us—unless we stop them now—while we still can."

"Did you hear what Borgman's orders were—after he'd wiped out the Hukk fleet?"

"No . . . and Tan—are you really sure that was what they intended? I can't—"

"Ask Daddy."

"You're being nasty."

"It's in the air. After Borgman and Veidt had cleaned up the Grand Armada—in what the reports would no doubt have described as a brilliantly fought action against a numerically superior foe—they planned a search-and-destroy sweep through the Arm, to weed out every last Hukk settlement, automated station, scientific installation and what have you. Then on to the home world. I don't know precisely what they had in mind once they got there—"

"You're exaggerating! You're making it sound terrible—like some sort of Mongol horde running amok!"

"Sure, it sounds a little rough. But with men of the caliber of Veidt and Borgman in charge we could all relax, knowing it was all for the best."

"Now you're descending to sarcasm. It's not like you, Tan. It's petty—and you were never petty."

"My ego's just had a severe blow. I discovered what kind of people I come from. It's depressing."

"Tan—you take it all too—too personally. You feel it too much." Arianne put her hand on his. "Come on, let's go somewhere and have a nice dinner and a few drinks and try to relax. You can't carry the whole load of the world on your shoulders."

Dalton looked at the girl—at her clear, wide eyes, her flawless complexion, at the rich luxuriance of her hair.

"You represent the top of the line," he said slowly. "The cream of the crop. You have intelligence, beauty, education; you have breeding, sensitivity, a fine, inquiring mind. If *you* don't see the point—"

"I see it, Tan. But I know there's a limit to the influence any one individual can have. I don't want to see you destroy yourself for nothing—for no effect."

"Have I destroyed myself? All I did was say 'no' to a senator."

"Daddy makes a poor enemy, Tan. If he thinks you're working against him, he'll fight you in every way he can. He believes in *his* ideas, too, you know."

Dalton nodded. "By the way—he tipped me off that I should drop you from my list. Just a gentle hint between practical men, you understand. For the good of the party. Or something."

"You've had too much to drink. Dad would never—" She broke off. "Oh, Tan, he *didn't* . . ."

"So—I think it might be best for you to allow me to call you a spinner, and—"

"I'm surprised. I didn't think you were afraid of Daddy—or of anything."

"I'm afraid of lots of things, Ari. The trick is not to let it influence your judgment too much."

"*I'm* not afraid of him," Arianne said. For a moment she looked into Dalton's eyes. Then she smiled, a faint and troubled smile. "Either," she added.

3

"I see by the morning 'casts," Deputy Secretary Treech said in a sleek tone, "that the Joint Chiefs were against any hasty action all along. The scurrilous rumors that have been circulated to the effect that secret orders were issued to attack the Hukk armada during the recent courtesy call are hotly denied." He cocked a bushy eyebrow at Dalton and sipped his coffee.

The morning breeze was gentle on the high balcony where Rear Admiral Dalton and the recently upgraded cabinet officer sat at breakfast. A delicate aroma of broiling bacon came from the preplate set into the center of a small, circular table. Distantly, music tinkled.

"Courtesy call," Dalton mused. "Why don't you call it what it was, Mr. Secretary: a sneak punch that didn't quite come off?"

Treech looked surprised, then disapproving. "I'm not sure I approve of that sort of joke, Dalton, even here. It's just the kind of remark that could be seized on and made much of in certain quarters."

"It wasn't intended as a joke."

"An unguarded utterance, then, if you will—"

"Mr. Secretary, you know what happened—and so do I. What's wrong with being factual about it?"

"There's no point in raking up past errors of judgment," Treech said stonily. "I've reached an understanding with our Hardlining admirals within the Department—"

"I wasn't thinking of publicizing the Kill order—"

"An unfortunate term."

"Uh-huh, an unfortunate idea—but they tried it. On the other hand, it offends the Softliners to be reminded—"

"Another unfortunate term, Dalton. I'd prefer to have you employ the term 'Moderates.' "

"It offends certain people that the Hukk were foolish enough to try what they did. That doesn't change the fact that they did it. If the public were fully informed—"

"Dalton, as a career officer, you certainly know better than to divulge any information—to make *any* public statement not previously cleared by BuPubRel!"

Dalton nodded. "My question was addressed to you, Mr. Secretary."

"Look here, Dalton—I don't like being baited. Now, I have plans for you. I suggest you put aside these pettifogging questions of yours and adopt an attitude more appropriate to the situation."

"Just what is the situation, Mr. Secretary? Since I pinned the extra star on two weeks ago, I've been kicking my heels in Washington—"

"I had an idea you'd appreciate a bit of relaxation. At the same time, I've been looking over various possible assignments for you." Treech gave Dalton a somber look, then allowed a small bland smile to twitch the corners of his mouth.

"Over a certain amount of opposition, I've decided to appoint you as a special aide to the Office of the

Assistant Secretary for Fleet Liaison Affairs." He waited with a comfortable expression.

"Sounds like the kind of job that's usually handed out to well-connected young comers who're being groomed to run for the Senate," Dalton commented.

"True, true. But I think you deserve it. Now, what I have in mind—"

"I don't think I'd fit in the job," Dalton said. "I'm a fleet man."

"Don't be stupidly modest, Dalton. The fleet is an anachronism; there's no future there. Already its role is being converted from the old aggressive image to that of a caretaker force—"

"So I've heard, Mr. Secretary. I thnk it's a major mistake."

"It so happens," Treech said ominously, "that I'm the principal architect of Conversion."

"I know that, Mr. Secretary. It's still a mistake."

"Look here, Dalton, you leave matters of Departmental policy to me and attend to carrying out your instructions. Don't let your new rank go to your head! You're still a very minor cog in a very large machine. It would behoove you to devote less time to these rather juvenile notions and more effort to determining how best to satisfy me."

"I hold my commission from the Council," Dalton said, "confirmed by the Senate. My oath is to the Constitution, not to any individual, however placed."

"Why, you're babbling like a child!" Treech said, looking astounded. "Do you realize, man, that I called you up here to hand you a plum—a job that half the flag officers of the Navy would give their retirement for? And you sit there and virtually spit in my face!"

"If you wanted a yes-man you shouldn't have called me."

Treech's fist hit the table. "None of your damned

insolence, Dalton! I selected you because I had confidence in you!"

"I don't want a ceremonial job, Mr. Secretary."

"Ceremonial, hell! You're going to play a major role in an upcoming campaign that's of more lasting importance than any conceivable amount of . . . of navigational sleight of hand!"

"What kind of campaign?"

"The draft Hukk treaty—which, as you know, I was instrumental in shaping—will be going nto committee in a matter of days. The reception it meets will depend on the correct manipulation of a number of sensitive factors—including that public opinion you were so concerned about a moment ago." Treech leaned back, took a deep breath, and let it out, making a show of calming himself.

"The treaty, as presently drafted," he went on, "will be a landmark in the history of enlightened alien policy. By disavowal of all taint of the punitive, it lays a basis for a complete reversal of our former oppressive relationship with the Hukk. I don't mind telling you that I've staked my personal prestige—my future in government—on its passage as proposed." Treech eyed the officer sternly. "If the Hardliners overturn this treaty—if Kelvin and his cronies can discredit the Moderate Hukk policy by forcing through a harsh treaty—well . . ." Treech's face was bleak. "It's not just a fight for the treaty, Dalton; it's a fight for the direction of Terran policy for decades to come."

"What's all this got to do with me, Mr. Secretary?"

"I'm getting to that," Treech snapped. "As a practical politician—and proud of it—I've been working with public image-making for almost thirty years." He frowned intently at Dalton.

"For the moment, we Moderates hold the upper hand; public-opinion-wise. When the Hardliners' gambit failed—because of my forethought in preparing you for the attempted coup—and I'm not minimizing your clever handling of the developing affair—when Veidt and Borgman and their clique were prevented from implementing their schemes for genocide—thanks largely to your stubbornness, I confess—it left them in a very awkward position. With your tapes, I was in position to clean house once and for all." Treech nodded his head solemnly, approving his actions. "But I didn't. Instead, I used the leverage to bring about certain understandings, to the advantage of all concerned. That's one of the primary lessons a true statesman learns, Dalton: never close a door. You never know when you may need an escape route."

"About this campaign—"

"I'm telling you! Getting a treaty through Congress isn't merely a matter of routine; my policy—and that of the Secretary himself, of course—"

"I'd almost forgotten we had one."

"The Secretary isn't a well man, Dalton. I'm glad to shoulder a part of the load. I have his complete confidence. Now, due to my handling of Departmental press releases, you're something of a national hero at the moment, Dalton. The populace sees you as a fearless warrior who stopped their favorite bugaboo at the threshold—nonsense, of course—and then showed magnanimity to a defeated foe. Frightful claptrap, but excellent Sunday tape stuff. Well, they need a colorful figure of romance to fasten their attention on. There's no harm in it—so long as you don't fall prey to the same delusion." Treech looked hard at Dalton.

"I intend to see this treaty confirmed," he said flatly, "It will face powerful opposition from several quarters—but we have plenty of weight on our side, too. You can do your bit by employing your moment in the limelight to help lead opinion in the proper direction."

"I see. And you'll be on hand to point out the direction."

"Exactly. Now, our own strictures against public utterances by active duty personnel will impose some limitations on your effectiveness, of course—or at least on the scope of the activities open to you. But there are plenty of ways in which you can exercise influence. Remarks dropped at private social affairs, for example; oblique implications insinuated into interviews on other matters entirely. And of course you'll be called on to testify before the committee. You'll know how to handle that. It's a matter of subtlety, finesse, the delicate touch. Any blatant politicking on your part, and a howl will go up from the Hardliners—including a large portion of the Navy brass—which would require action by the Department. Naturally, I don't want that."

"Naturally."

Treech looked sharply at Dalton. "At times I wonder about you, Dalton. Certainly you proved yourself ideologically when you refused to carry out the massacre—although even there you seem to have had some reservations. The requirement for stripping the Hukk vessels of their armaments, for example—most humiliating to Admiral Saanch'k. I suppose it was intended as a placating gesture toward French and the others, and as such, defensible tactics, but there's no room for divided loyalties now. You've made implacable enemies of the Hardline party within the Naval High Command. Your only future lies with the Moderates. We may as well have that clear at the outset."

"You put it plainly enough, Mr. Secretary," Dalton said.

"Very well, then. In your new job I'll expect you to carry out your duties with the same zeal as you apply to ordinary military assignments. You understand the objective, and the dangers. See that you take them into account, and conduct yourself accordingly."

"I may be a big disappointment to you, Mr. Secretary. I'm not very good at cocktail party conversation."

"Don't be concerned about that; my Placprop people have prepared an extensive briefing for you. You'll be fed lines suitable for any contingency. You need merely learn to curb your tongue and say the right thing as opportunity offers, and I'll be well satisfied."

"I still think you're going to be disappointed."

"You'd be surprised how much weight your opinions seem to have with the public, Dalton. Play your cards close to your chest, and I can see that third star for you in the statutory minimum time."

4

"I don't see what there is to be grim about, darling," Arianne said. "It's just like an extended leave here in Washington—and plenty of dazzling social events to keep you from getting bored. Of course old Tubby Treech will be peeking over your shoulder, making sure you don't say anything out of line, but that's a small price to pay."

"Sure," Dalton said.

The girl, sitting relaxed on a low, wide divan beside the fireplace in which a genuine wood fire burned, shedding a soft light but little heat, looked at him for a long moment.

"This seems to be one of those situations you can feel developing," she said carefully. "There's nothing you can put your finger on, exactly; but it hangs in the air, getting thicker and clammier and colder in spite of anything we can say or do." She took a quick sip of her wine and put the glass down. Her cheeks were flushed now, her eyes bright.

"Damn! Does it have to be this way? Are we so helpless that we can't stop it, make everything the way it ought to be? The way it used to be?"

"I don't know," Dalton said expressionlessly.

"I won't ask you if you don't care," Arianne said, her voice harsh now. "I know you do. But you don't care enough—or in the right way—or . . ." She broke off and quite suddenly was crying. Dalton got up and went to her, pressed her head to his shoulder.

"Sorry, girl," he said softly. "It's not you; maybe it's not even me."

She looked up at him, her expression taut, hungry. "Tan—we're not leaves, floating downstream. We're people—intelligent, aware, reasoning beings. We've had—still have something between us that's valuable, not easy to find. Let's not let anything destroy it. Not this silly assignment, not Daddy, not—anything."

"Not my damn fool stubbornness, you mean," Dalton said, not bitterly. "The funny think is, I know exactly what you mean. If anyone had asked me if I'd ever let a bunch of abstract ideas come between me and my girl, I'd have laughed at him. But—the way they come at you, Ari—the way it creeps up, an inch today, an inch tomorrow, until you're up to your neck and no way to go back . . ."

"I know—damn it. You won't sit still for it—you can't—and that's because you're the man I love—or you're the man I love because you're that way—or I love you because you're the kind of man that won't be led, or pushed, or conned or bought."

"Sure I can. I bought the Navy a long time ago, the whole program. Something clean and honest to believe in, the comradeship of men you admired and respected, the ideals and the tradition, a clear-cut choice between what's good and true, and . . . the rest of it. It sounds trite and naive now, but it didn't when I was sixteen years old, getting that Academy appointment."

"That's not the same—"

"Sure it is. I bought a dream—a set of illusions. But the funny thing about a set of illusions is that they can be true—they *are* true—if you believe them. And I believed them. I still do—in an abstract sort of way—the way it *could* be. If only . . ."

"That's it: if only. If only this whole rotten Hukk business didn't exist; if only there weren't pressures on you that you can't yield to, and other pressures on me that I can't defy. But—Tan—" She sat up and looked at him. "There has to be some method of dealing with the realities of life, and the Navy, and politics and the pressures of society—without being destroyed in the process. A way to *win* instead of having to choose between going down gloriously in flames or selling your soul to the devil."

"It seems simple enough to me," Dalton said, frowning. "If we faced the truth—dealt with reality as it is—"

"But—don't you see, Tan? Reality is different for different people. Dad really and truly believes that the Hukk will destroy us unless we destroy them. He sees any softness toward them as indefensible folly, if not outright villainy. And he's not striking a pose, Tan. He *believes* it!"

"And he may be right," Dalton said. "I can't prove he isn't."

"And Secretary Treech: he thinks his way is right—"

"I wouldn't count on it. It's become a political article of faith with him. He committed himself to the Softline—"

"Because at some level he believes in it. If not him, then most of his followers. They look back on our record of mistreatment of savages and weaker nations, and they're determined not to repeat the crimes of the past. They feel just as strongly as Daddy—I realize that—"

"How do *you* feel, personally?"

"I . . . I'm not well enough informed to really have an opinion that means anything, Tan. I've been subjected to Hardline propaganda since I was a child. I was raised to think of the Hukk as villains, ugly, alien outlaws and opportunists, shrewdly and cynically picking our brains for all they can get—so they can use it against us. But . . . as I grew up, I began to wonder, to doubt. Lots of my friends at school had had just the opposite background. They were convinced that the Hukk are earnest, kindly, decent, with the same hopes and dreams as we have—and that we, as a superpower, were suppressing them, denying them their birthright."

"What do you believe today?"

"Well—they *did* try their sneak attack on Luna. If it hadn't been for you, they'd probably have succeeded. I can't square *that* with the image of a sweet, peace-loving race."

"They were out to grab all they could, there's no doubt about that," Dalton said.

"But on the other hand—Borgman's scheme—to bombard their fleet after it had surrendered—that's vile, unspeakable. Nothing could excuse such an act. So . . ." She shrugged, smiled a perplexed smile. "What do I believe? Am I a Hardliner or a Softliner?"

"I think giving things names is part of the problem," Dalton said. "The implication is that you have to be one or the other."

"But, Tan—if you don't commit yourself—if you don't take a stand one way or another—you're nothing. You're a cipher; you don't count in the final analysis. That's what Daddy says—and I think he's right. It's no good saying 'gray' if the choice is black or white. It's like abstaining."

"That's nonsense," Dalton said. "Tired old nonsense. It's a two-valued solution to an infinitely complex problem. But it makes things easier all around. You don't have to think. Just close your eyes and stab."

Arianne's smile was tense and strained now. "You paint me as a gullible dupe, and my father a totalitarian villain—but I'm not going to let you impose any such simple two-valued solution on the problem of our infinitely complex relationship." Two tears welled from her eyes and ran down her cheeks.

"Don't pay any attention to that," she said coolly. "Unfortunately, I have no control over the autonomic functions of the body I inhabit."

"Ari, you're worth any hundred head of politicos chosen at random—Human or Hukk. I don't really give a damn about helping any power clique take control. What I'd like to see is a general recognition of the realities of the situation, an ability to deal with what *is,* instead of what somebody hopes, or wishes, or fears, or imagines—some arbitrary guess they've staked a career on, or some article of ideology. Is that too much to ask? Why does your father ignore the fact that the Hukk, like any life form, will naturally respond to the instinct to move into what looks to them like a power vacuum—and not hate them for it, just recognize it, and deal with it? Why can't Treech and his Softliners realize that the Hukk aren't a band of angels? That they'll naturally grab anything that looks like it's lying around to be grabbed?"

"I don't know why they don't see things as you do, Tan," Arianne said soberly. "Of course, you're assuming that the way you see them is the right way, that everybody else is wrong—"

"There might be a few people here and there that agree with me," Dalton said.

"I wouldn't count on it, Tan. People are funny that way. They take stands; they give their loyalties. They feel strongly about things."

"And I don't?"

"I didn't say that, did I? They pick their heroes—as they've picked you—the noble, truehearted man who saved them from the enemy, and then showed gallantry to a defeated foe. They liked that, Tan. They're really rather romantic, the ordinary people—the ones who produce something for a living, rather than manipulating the product of other people's efforts."

"That one missed me."

"You didn't build the fleet, Tan. Your life's earnings couldn't pay for a side boat. Not just you—the Navy. Politicians, too. My father—myself, secondhand: I've lived well all my life, eaten the best of foods, worn the best clothes, attended the best schools —all on the taxpayers' money. But I try not to fool myself. I've had a soft life, and I've enjoyed it. I'm not one for sackcloth and ashes. I don't feel guilty— not in the least. And neither does Daddy—why should he? They can vote him out any time. And neither should you. You're doing a job that needs doing, and the public is perfectly willing to pay for that job. And to idolize you when you do something that strikes some sort of responsive chord. But you must remember—all of us must remember—that we're really small, powerless creatures as individuals—"

"Negative," Dalton said. "If I believed that I'd have quit a long time ago."

"But that's just what I'm getting at, Tan! You have an . . . arrogance—a conviction that somehow *your* ideas, your view of things is the only correct one—"

"I'm willing to be convinced otherwise—but not by a political payoff—or by the baying of a pack of wet-hanky do-gooders hot on the scent of a worthy cause."

"Payoff, Tan? There are those who might interpret your promotion as something of the sort—and some of them are saying so."

Dalton nodded. He got to his feet. "I see," he said tightly. The girl stood quickly.

"I'm sorry, Tan, I didn't mean that the way it sounded. I was only trying to point out that anything—"

"Sure," Dalton said. "I'm going somewhere and take a bath."

"Tan—you can't leave like this! I only wanted—"

"I know. You want to make things simple and sweet—but they're not. And working out a set of euphemisms for it isn't going to help."

"Euphemisms? Is that what you call trying to talk reason instead of plunging ahead over whatever cliff it is you're heading for?" She caught his hand. "Tan—be careful. Don't try to cure the world single-handed. You can't do it. All you'll do is get yourself crushed in the gears."

"This week I've already resisted the temptation to punch a cabinet officer in the eye and stuff a senator's collected speeches down his throat. I'll try to continue to play it smooth."

"It's only for a little while, Tan. Once the treaty is through, attention won't be so focused on you."

"And I'll be back pounding a beat where I belong —if we have any Navy left then."

CHAPTER SEVEN

"Now, my boy," Assistant Secretary Treech said, and smiled a smile which Dalton thought didn't come across in person quite as well as it televised. "There's nothing for you to be nervous about. The committee is by no means hostile toward you personally—and I have it on good authority they fully intend to report the treaty favorably within a day or two. Your testimony will merely serve to confirm one or two points, lend a touch of interest to the press coverage prior to the announcement." Treech let the smile drop and assumed a sober, judicial look.

"I must say that I've been disappointed that you haven't found more opportunity in the past weeks to put in a word here and there in support of our position—but I suppose it could be argued that a certain appearance of discretion was advisable in the long run."

When Dalton said nothing, Treech hurried on. "As I say, the fight is all but won; so merely look them in the eye—the tough old space-dog approach, the simple man of action, you know the routine. Tell them what they want to hear, pose for a few snaps—and you're done." Treech manipulated the wrinkles around his eyes to give an effect of benign playfulness. "And I think you can look forward to a new assignment in the near future, of an importance consonant with your services to me—to the Department, that is to say." He rose and extended a large, well-tended hand.

"Good luck, Admiral. We'll all be watching you and wishing you well."

The other functionaries gathered in the Assistant Secretary's office stepped forward to add their murmured words. Dalton shook half a dozen hands before he was able to escape into the corridor. An SP escort was waiting to convey him to the Capitol. Strobe lights popped; photographers shouted peremptory orders to look their way. Dalton bulldozed through them, through the crowd in the hearing room, to the table where ranked microphones and cameras waited. There was more handshaking.

"Nice crowd," a senatorial aide leaned to say to Dalton as he took his seat. "They've come to hear and see you, of course, Admiral. You're quite the popular figure." He was a slickly groomed youngish man, immaculately tailored, and he smelled of an expensive cologne. Dalton grunted and leaned away from the odor. The youngish man went on talking in a glib, confidential tone, pointing out celebrities. It was very noisy in the big room; there was an air of hectic activity, like picnickers threatened by a storm. People hurried to and fro; people went into huddles; voices crackled over the PA system, with cryptic announcements. Gradually the room settled down. A last messenger scuttled past, and near-silence fell.

A monkey-faced old senator named Ketchum, from

Iowa, was chairing the hearing. "It was good of you to come here today, Admiral," he stated formally.

As if I had any choice in the matter, Dalton thought. *Why do we go through these forms? They know I was ordered here, and they know I know they know—and so on, ad nauseam. Empty rituals. Who is it we're trying to fool? Ourselves? Must be, there's nobody else. . . .*

". . . here today to clear up a number of points in regard to the incident of last month in which you played a prominent part. I refer, of course, to the matter of the detachment of the Hukk fleet encountered in the vicinity of Luna." Ketchum was merely reading routine data into the record, Dalton knew; he listened absently.

". . . idea has been expressed that the presence of foreign warships in Home Space in itself constituted an inimical act, however doubtful that may be. I think all of us here today agree that your actions, Admiral, showed commendable restraint. . . ."

Arianne is probably here somewhere, Dalton thought. *The place is packed. Plenty of interest in the treaty. Everybody's concerned about the Hukk, one way or another, wanting to do the right thing. Most of them have no facts to go on, though, except what's served up to them via the press: government handouts, pronouncements by politicos with a program to sell, strident opinions by tri-di actors, astrologers and givers of advice to the lovelorn. Too bad there isn't some way of recording the data and presenting it, cold turkey, for every reasoning man to draw his own conclusions from. But—*

". . . your opinion, Admiral, as to whether, in fact, the Hulk admiral actually intended to launch an attack against this planet?" Dalton tuned in on the words. The aide inconspicuously adjusted the microphone a bit closer to him.

"No, sir," Dalton said.

Ketchum nodded. "Now, Admiral, did in fact any, ah, overtly hostile action by the Hukk vessels take place? Assuming, for the moment, that is, that their presence in itself did not constitute such an act."

"No, sir."

"In your considered opinion as a professional officer and a student of military affairs—an expert, I might say, in such matters—did the Hukk fleet you encountered possess the capability of launching any *militarily* effective attack against this planet?"

"No, sir, it did not."

"Would you say, sir, that the Hukk admiral was the type of, ah, individual given to hasty, ill-thought-out actions? Of committing himself to capricious, spur-of-the-moment adventures?"

"No, sir."

"Would there be any advantage, in your view, that the Hukk might have obtained—military, psychological, propaganda or what have you—from such an attack on this planet?"

"None."

"It's your opinion then, Admiral, that the intentions of the Hukk fleet were entirely peaceful?"

"No, sir."

"And—" Ketchum broke off, his bland expression changing to one of surprise. In the momentary silence, strobe lights wink-winked.

"If I rephrase that, Admiral," Ketchum said gingerly. "What I'm getting at is, is it your opinion that the Hukk had no hostile intent in venturing into so-called Home Space—that in fact—"

"No, sir, that's not my opinion."

A babble of voices started up. People were rising

to crane at Dalton. Ketchum was looking sharply at him. The man beside him—Senator Baldrum from Minnesota, Dalton thought—put his mouth to Ketchum's ear and spoke urgently. Ketchum nodded. He shuffled papers. Someone cleared his throat loudly.

"Perhaps you'd tell us then, Admiral, just what it was you feel the Hukk had in mind."

An expectant silence settled. Dalton remembered Arianne's face as he had seen it last.

"Tan . . . don't try to cure the world single-handed. . . ."

"I can only offer conjecture on that point, Senator," Dalton said.

"Quite right," one of the committee members spoke up, in a deep, sonorous voice. "The admiral is here today to testify only as regarding matters of which he has personal knowledge. His opinions and speculations, while interesting, are not germane to the issue at hand."

"Admiral Dalton, during the period preceding the recent fleet exercise," Ketchum hurried on, "rumors were rife to the effect that the Hukk were in process of assembling a fleet—a massive buildup of military forces in the vicinity of the, ah"—he raked through his notes—"the Piranha System. Was there, in fact, any such buildup?"

"Not to my knowledge."

"Isn't it a fact that the only Hukk vessels found to be operating in that volume of space were small, unarmed scientific vessels carrying out electronic experimentation programs?"

"No, sir."

"What's that?" Ketchum's head came up sharply.

"The ships were small and unarmed as you said, sir. But they were not engaged in electronic experiments. They were fully operational."

"Indeed. Well, we're not here to nit-pick, Admiral. The point is, I'm sure you'll agree, they were inoffensive, non-combatant-type vessels."

"That depends on the scope of your definition of those terms, Senator. A spy is inoffensive, in the sense that he doesn't carry a rifle—"

"You're saying they were spy ships? I'd like to know just what it was they were spying on, out in that remote region of space."

"That's not what I said, Senator—"

"I think my hearing is unimpaired, in spite of my years, Admiral! You've implied that these small ships —three in number, I believe, were engaged in spying —or in some other presumably unfriendly activity— out there in the Piranha System. Inasmuch as we have no interests in that area whatever, I'd like for you to tell this committee, Admiral, just what sort of threat you imagine they posed."

"Just a moment." The deep-voiced committee member spoke up again. "With all respect, Senator—I must object to any pursual of matters which the admiral might, ah, 'imagine,' as you put it. We're not here today to listen to imaginings. We want facts, nothing more."

"Well, now, as to that," a small, nervous-looking committeeman said, "I think perhaps the chairman was employing a figure of speech. After all, Admiral Dalton didn't say they posed a threat. I believe he pointed out that they were fully operational units. I'd like to know what their mission was?"

"Electronics subterfuge," Dalton said. "Decoy work."

"Just what does that mean?"

"The ships were fitted out with gear that enabled them to create the illusion that they were a whole fleet."

"For what purpose?"

"To make us think their fleet was there."

"For what purpose?"

"If it was there, presumably it wasn't somewhere else—en route to Sol, for example."

"Just a minute, Admiral. We've wandered back into the area of conjecture again. I must insist that it's the purpose of this committee to study the *facts*—not someone's guesswork—however educated that guess might be."

"Was there, Admiral," Ketchum said severely, "any way in which these three vessels could have inflicted any damage on Terran property?"

"Not directly."

"Now, it's my understanding that when called upon by you to assume Lunar orbit," Ketchum went on quickly, "Admiral Saanch'k immediately complied with your request. Is that correct?"

"There was a certain amount of discussion—"

"Within a matter of fifteen minutes, according to your own official report, Admiral!" Ketchum snapped.

"My report was accurate."

"Having shown his peaceful intentions by thus complying with what might ordinarily have been considered a somewhat provocative request—Admiral Saanch'k then permitted Terran Naval personnel to board vessels of his command to satisfy themselves that these vessels were unarmed. Does that agree with your recollection, Admiral?"

"Your wording implies—"

"Never mind my wording, Admiral. Did the Hukk admiral enter the holding orbit specified, did he allow Naval personnel to board his ships, did they or did they not certify that the vessels were unarmed on their departure, yes or no?"

"I see," Dalton said. "You ask the questions and supply the answers too. That being the case, you don't need me." He rose.

"Admiral—you'll resume your seat, or I'll hold you in contempt of Congress!" Ketchum howled.

"Ah, Admiral"—another committee member spoke up—"I'm sure we can resolve this small difficulty—if you'd be kind enough to resume your seat—" His voice was drowned out in the rising hubbub. Dalton was still standing beside his chair. A face in the audience behind a velvet barrier rope caught his eye. For a moment he thought it was Arianne; but it was a stranger, a pretty girl with large, dark eyes, staring solemnly at him. Aided by gavel pounding, the noise subsided.

"Well, Admiral?" Ketchum's voice grated.

"Senator," Dalton said, "it's my duty to give you as clear and factual a picture of the matter as possible. I don't intend to be put in the position of appearing to be substantiating a distorted version of what happened out there."

The murmur that rose and quickly died had a shocked quality. Dalton allowed the expectant stillness to stretch out for another few moments.

"I therefore suggest," he said, "that you allow me to briefly state the facts of the matter."

"Admiral, I'm conducting this hearing—" Ketchum started, then paused again, leaning to hear a comment addressed to him by a man on his left. He frowned judiciously, shuffled his papers. The crowd was very quiet.

"This committee is not here to listen to rambling reminiscences," Ketchum said, "but to ascertain the facts regarding specific points—"

"If you're not here to get the whole truth," Dalton cut in, "you've got no business being here at all."

Ketchum gaveled the outburst of talk into silence.

"Admiral, I could hold you in contempt—" he started, then pounded again for silence. The committee members conferred again. Ketchum nodded, as if reluctantly.

"All right, Admiral," he said. "I suppose I should make allowances for the fact that you're unaccustomed to parliamentary procedures. If you'll kindly take your seat and permit this hearing to proceed—"

"I can say what I have to say standing up, Senator. You were questioning me about the intentions of the Hukk Grand Armada—"

"You can spare us any jingoistic terminology," Ketchum barked. "And you'll limit your comments to matters already brought up in the preceding discussion."

"You asked me what the Hukk were doing here," Dalton said. "They entered Solar space for the purpose of seizing Fortress Luna."

This time Ketchum had to threaten to clear the room before the uproar reluctantly subsided.

"You've made a recklessly inflammatory statement, Admiral," he called over the fading babble. "A statement totally unsubstantiated by any evidence whatever!"

"Just a minute." Another committeeman spoke up. He stared at Dalton with a thoughtful frown. "If the Hukk intended to attack Luna, Admiral—why didn't they proceed to do so?"

"Because Admiral Saanch'k became convinced it wouldn't be a good idea."

"When only minutes from the target? Rather late in the game for such a sweeping change of heart, wasn't it, Admiral?"

"Not too late."

"What changed their minds?"

"They hadn't expected to meet any resistance."

"Really?" Ketchum said with a note of triumph. "According to the record, Admiral—including your own statements—the only force in the vicinity was your own rather modest flotilla. Are you suggesting that Admiral Saanch'k was frightened off by a detachment a quarter the size of his own?"

"He was under the impression the entire fleet was in attack position."

"Oh? Now, isn't it a fact, Admiral, that the fleet was at that time actually very distant from the System?"

"That's right."

"Can you suggest how the Hukk commander—by your own statement, a capable officer—came to be so grossly misinformed about the disposition of the very force which, if your contention were true, would be his primary concern?"

"I gave him the idea," Dalton said.

"So? That isn't mentioned in the official transcript of the fleet report. Are you saying the report is falsified? That's quite an accusation to make against your own superiors, Admiral!"

"The report's accurate, as far as it goes. But a few things were left out."

"Such as your own rather dramatic role in the affair," Baldrum suggested.

"I wouldn't put it quite that way."

"You say, then, that the Hukk dispatched this giant war fleet here to attack us, and gave up the scheme when you appeared on the scene."

"That's about it."

"They simply gave up—in spite of the obvious inferiority of the forces at your command?"

"I've already explained that."

"Oh, yes. You simply told the Hukk admiral he was outnumbered."

"That's right."

"In other words, you lied to him," a female committee member said in a penetrating voice.

"I suppose you could say that."

"So—having frightened the Hukk fleet into giving up the objective of what must have been, according to your own statement, a massively expensive and carefully planned assault—with unarmed ships, mind you—"

"They were fully armed," Dalton cut in.

"You testified a moment ago that inspection teams went aboard the vessels and certified that they were in fact incapable of firing a shot!"

"That's right—after the demolition teams disarmed them."

"That's quite a picture you paint, Admiral," Ketchum grated. "Instead of the incursion of a number of unarmed Hukk vessels—I don't believe the exact number is mentioned in the brief of the Fleet Action Report—you ask us to believe that in fact a giant fleet of warships, bristling with armament and hell-bent on attack, was halted in its tracks—disarmed, and sent on its way—by you. A remarkable performance, Admiral." His voice become sardonic. "What a pity that there's nothing in the record so far made available to us—absolutely nothing—to substantiate it."

"That's easy enough to correct, Senator. Every fleet vessel is equipped with automatic continuous recording gear. I suggest you subpoena the recordings from my flagship."

"Very well; that will be done," Ketchum said grumpily. He glanced at his fellow committee members.

"I'm adjourning this hearing until these records are made available to us. That's all, Admiral Dalton." He looked at him with a bleak expression. "We'll examine these claims of your more closely tomorrow, sir. I suggest you examine your recollections and make quite certain that you haven't allowed your memory of events to become confused in the weeks of public scrutiny you've enjoyed since the event."

2

"What are you trying to do, Tan, sink the Navy? Strike back at some of those old dodos with too many stars who don't run things just the way you'd prefer? Or is it yourself you're out to get? If so, I think you've done it very nicely." Arianne threw down the glove she had been twisting between her fingers and gave Dalton a fierce look.

"Funny," Dalton said, "I went up there fully intending to be a good little boy and concur in some routinely hoked-up version of the matter that would show how the Joint Chiefs had known about the Hukk scheme all along, and how Borgman and Veidt had planned the whole thing. It even occurred to me I might be in line for a favorable mention." He shook his head. "But not this. Not a whitewash job designed to make Saanch'k and his battlewagons look like a detachment of picnickers who got roughed up by the big, bad policeman—"

"Now who's exaggerating? They *could* have painted you as a hothead who almost started a war—but they didn't. They covered up parts of it that would have made the Navy look foolish. All right—it's an old custom, Tan, and we both know it. But there was nothing unfavorable about you in the official version. Nothing to alter the public's picture of you as their Man of the Hour. There are a number of ranking admirals who'd have been glad to throw you to the dogs, Tan—

but that didn't happen. True, you didn't get credit for what you really did—"

"Do you think that's what's bothering me?"

"No—not really. But—"

"Damn it, woman, do you think that has *any* bearing on what I told those senators?"

"Don't swear at me, Tan."

"Answer my question."

"I . . . no, I know it doesn't. I was being nasty—deliberately. A little revenge for your being such a fool, such a big, noble, high-minded, idiotic *fool!*"

"You think it's foolish to try to tell the truth—"

"It is when you don't have the ghost of a chance of being believed!"

"They'll play the tapes tomorrow. It's all there."

"Tan—are you really sure . . . was the FAR really *that* distorted?"

"I only saw excerpts—the parts I had to authenticate. They were correct."

Arianne rubbed her wrists together slowly, as if her hands were cold. "I don't understand. Why would they be so foolish as to publish such a fabrication if the record won't bear them out?"

"I suppose they didn't expect to be challenged."

"It's such a twisted, complicated situation. The Secretary virtually a figurehead, the Assistant a fervent Softliner, half the senior admirals confirmed Hardliners, and the rest set to jump either way—and you caught in the middle. Oh, Tan—I don't see how this can end in any way that will . . . that will let us . . ."

"Try to understand, Ari. Regardless of what the Hardliners think and what the Softliners hope, the Hukk have demonstrated their intentions. They tipped their hand, and we got a good, hard look at it. We can't afford to ignore what we saw. We can't bury it in the files and proceed as if it had never happened.

Those senators have to know that the Hukk sent their Grand Armada in here loaded for bear—and they have to shape their treaty accordingly. Apparently, nobody's going to mention the fact if I don't. So I have to. It's that simple."

"What about the Hardline admirals? They'd love to see the Hukk painted as villains—"

"Uh-huh—maybe. But the boys made a bad move when they planned their little take-over coup that didn't work out. That gave Treech what he needed. He was hinting about it, but I didn't know what he meant at the time. But it was a simple deal. The FAR went out in the form he dictated—and Veidt and Borgman and a few others kept their jobs."

"It all sounds so . . . venal."

"As you pointed out, the Softliners believe in their theory. They know what ought to be true, and they're willing to face up to the necessity for editing reality a little so as not to give wrong ideas to the impressionable."

"But—to suppress news of an attempted attack, Tan! To falsify official reports, to lie to Congress—"

"The Navy has the only actual records; who's to check up on them? If they say there were only a dozen pleasure boats out there, that's it—as long as nobody spills the beans."

"And you think you have to be the one to spill them."

"Who else can you suggest for the job?"

"Nobody, of course. But, Tan—why are you so convinced that Treech is wrong? Maybe he's right; maybe the correct course *is* to cover it up, not let any popular hysteria develop, give the Hukk an easy peace—"

"He's wrong."

"He's your superior. Why is it up to you to challenge him?"

"I'd like to see a disaster averted."

"You think Treech would pursue the policy he does if he thought it would end in disaster? He's not a stupid man. It's not to his advantage to encourage Hukk military adventures."

"Maybe he half-believes his line, and maybe he's thinking about next year's Council elections—and how sick he and his Softline would look if word got out that the Hukk made a play for Luna."

"What good would election do him if the Hukk blow Washington off the map? And what makes you think he's so totally devoid of decency as to be willing to plunge us into war, just to win an election?"

"I don't think Treech believes the Hukk pose any real threat. After he's elected, he can always shift his position a few points at a time and end up being the clear-sighted leader who knew it all along."

"You're very cynical, aren't you, Tan?"

"I don't think so. Is it cynical of the fox to know the hunter's after him and take steps accordingly?"

"That's what I'm asking you to do, Tan. The hounds will be baying on your trail. You've called the JCS and the High Command liars; you've made the committee look like gullible ninnies. If you go up there tomorrow and make it worse—"

"What do you want me to do, Ari? Tell them it was just a slip of the tongue?"

"I don't know." She looked at him with wide, frightened eyes. "I don't know what I want you to do."

CHAPTER EIGHT

The hearing room was even more crowded today, Dalton saw as he took his place, but quieter. A group of ranking Naval officers came in and took seats silently at the rear. Borgman and Veidt were among them. Promptly at one o'clock the doors were closed and Ketchum silenced the murmur of conversation with a single rap of the hammer.

"Now, Admiral Dalton," he said after the routine announcement opening the hearing, "to return to certain specific points made yesterday by you. You stated, I believe, that the Hukk convoy which approached Home Space last month was in fact not a small and unarmed detachment but was a vast war fleet—a 'Grand Armada,' I believe was the term you employed. And that this armada was en route to launch an all-out attack against our installation on the moon but were dissuaded by yourself." He looked at Dalton as if peering over bifocals. "Is that correct?"

"Substantially."

"Now, this hostile fleet—outweighing the forces at your command by a factor of some four to one—on receiving your warning, immediately changed their plans and peacefully permitted members of the Space Arm to board their vessels and to incapacitate their armaments. Correct?"

"More or less."

"Now, Admiral, at the time you were carrying out this remarkable single-handed feat—were you acting under competent official orders?"

"I acted on my own initiative under the authority of a Departmental Special Order."

"I see. Now, who was your immediate commander at the time?"

"Prior to my detachment from the fleet—"

"Oh, you were detached from the fleet, you say. By whose order?"

"My own."

"Isn't that somewhat unusual, Admiral? I understood the fleet was under the command of Fleet Admiral Starbird."

"That's right—"

"Now, I confess I'm not a military man," Ketchum cut in, "but as I understand it, a commodore—your rank at the time—is several large rungs under a fleet admiral."

"That's common knowledge."

"Yet you maintain that at the time of your alleged, ah, disarming of this invading war fleet, you were in fact not acting under any orders but your own."

"I was acting under the general authority of a DSO, as I said."

"This Special Order directed you to absent yourself from the main body of the fleet and proceed to the vicinity of Luna?"

"Not specifically."

"Nevertheless, you did so, is that correct?"

"I never made rendezvous with the fleet—"

"Don't quibble, Admiral. You've said that you proceeded to Lunar space entirely on your own initiative, without being directed to do so."

"That's right."

"May I ask what led you to take this step?"

"I was advised by a vessel of my command that an unidentified convoy was approaching Luna. I turned back to intercept it."

"And how did it happen that a unit of your command was in position to detect such an intrusion, which passed unnoticed by any other unit of the fleet?"

"He was closer to the action."

"A straggler?"

"I'd sent him back to Boge for maintenance."

"The vessel in question was in need of repair?"

"That's what the depot was supposed to determine."

Ketchum picked up a paper and studied it. "The vessel in question was under the command of Captain Hunneker, is that correct?"

"That's right."

"According to the report I have here, Captain Hunneker's command had just been released from drydock at the fleet depot at Aldo, certified as fully spaceworthy and cleared for unlimited service."

"Nevertheless, I sent him back."

"You'd inspected the vessel and determined that the depot certification was in error?"

"No."

"Then would you mind telling me why you sent a spaceworthy fleet boat of the Navy out of action on a nugatory errand?"

"I wanted him to monitor circum-Terran space for signs of a Hukk sneak play."

"Ah—so you had evidence that such a, er, 'sneak play,' as you call it, was imminent?"

"No tangible evidence."

"What sort of evidence if not tangible, Admiral?"

"It seemed like a logical development."

Ketchum nodded gravely. "So you might say that you acted on a hunch, eh?"

"You might."

Ketchum was still nodding. "You're a remarkable man, Admiral. First, you have a hunch that a Hukk armada is about to attack Luna; then you single-handedly render it impotent." He looked up, an expression that was almost a smile on his face.

"Now you see it—now you don't," he remarked cheerfully, and abruptly glowered. His fist hit the table.

"Isn't it a fact, Admiral, that you were ordered to return to Luna for the express purpose of investigating the detachment of Hukk vessels whose position had been well known to Naval Intelligence for some time? That your instructions were to assure yourself that the vessels were in fact unarmed merchantmen; that you carried out your instructions, no more, no less—and that this entire story of a vast battle-ready invasion fleet is a complete fabrication!"

Dalton's denial was almost lost in the uproar that followed. Ketchum pounded in vain for a full minute while strobes winked and sound booms tracked over the crowd.

"All right," his voice penetrated at last. "Any more such outbursts and I'll clear the room."

In the corridor outside the committee room, Dalton encountered Admiral Veidt, his dress uniform and decorations resplendent in the gloomy setting. He was flanked by a covey of lesser ranks like a dreadnought convoyed by a horde of tenders.

"You're quite a boy, aren't you, Dalton?" Veidt inquired in the same genial tone that a hangman might employ in asking if the rope is comfortable.

A reporter, one of a large contingent awaiting targets of opportunity, pushed up beside Dalton.

"Admiral, do I correctly understand that you claim that Fleet Command was hoaxed totally off balance and out of position by the Hukk—taken in completely by a feint that allowed them to place an attack force in position to assault Luna or even Terra itself with impunity but that you, acting on your own initiative, saved the day?"

"No, that's not what I said," Dalton replied crisply. "There is some important information to be communicated to the committee and the public. I don't want to see it distorted to make a more sensational story. Please get it right."

"Very well, Admiral. Just what is this important message?"

"It's quite simple: the Hukk are not the simple, semi-civilized tribesmen they've been portrayed as in the media, helped along by official CDT handouts to the effect that they're a peace-loving mercantile people and in any event would represent a negligible opponent in the event of hostilities."

"You disagree?"

"Emphatically. They've established themselves in their home system as absolute masters—and have engulfed a number of nearby independent worlds. They're capable and deadly warriors, aggressive and tenacious—and they have their collective eye on Terran holdings in the Sirenian Sector, to begin with."

"In that case, Admiral, what course of action on our part do you recommend?"

"The recent 'exercise' was a step in the right direction, as far as it went. We showed them that we own a fleet of combat-ready vessels at least equal to their own. And by great good luck we aborted their first serious stab at us."

"Luck, Admiral? I understood you to say it was your own wisdom, foresight, and prompt action that saved the day."

"I don't think I used any of those words."

"Well, oh, not literally. But you implied—"

"I stated quite plainly, I think, that the Hukk are a menace not to be treated lightly."

"So—what course do you recommend, sir?" the reporter persisted.

"I suggest that it's important that we publicly recognize their recent gambit for the open act of war that it was, and respond accordingly."

"Launch an all-out counterattack, you mean, Admiral?"

"By no means. Their thrust was stopped. Their immediate ambitions have been thwarted; that's sufficient military reaction for the moment."

"Then what kind of reaction do you have in mind, sir?"

"The terms of the Hukk-Terran treaty now under preparation must embody the realities of the relationships between the two races."

"You're coming out in support of the Hardline position, Admiral?"

"You don't need me to talk to, mister. You seem to be making up your own answers faster than I can talk. Just don't attribute your guesses to me."

"Dalton." Admiral Veidt spoke up. "I'll tell you candidly that when you took your flotilla out of the line in the face of what looked like an impending action, I placed a rather negative interpretation on it.

You must agree it seemed you were turning tail in the face of the enemy; however, I fully approve of your subsequent handling of the intruding forces under Saanch'k. Up to a point that is—the point where you interfered with Admiral Borgman's carrying out of his instructions to neutralize the enemy fleet. There was considerable pressure on us at Fleet HQ to offer an apology for your interference and escort the Hukk vessels on their way.

"Happily a more realistic view prevailed," Veidt continued. "I was somewhat disturbed, however, Admiral, by some of your testimony before the committee. There seemed to be a clear implication, as the gentlemen of the press have sensed, that high command was remiss, negligent, and incompetent in its handling of the incident and that you alone averted a major disaster."

"It wasn't my intention, sir, to inflate my role in the matter; I merely wanted to make it crystal clear that a serious breach of the peace had occurred."

"There's another matter, Dalton, which will be the subject of a board of inquiry to be convened by me as soon as the committee dismisses you."

"I assume you refer to the rather incoherent orders I received and disregarded."

"You admit openly that you disregarded competent orders?"

"As I interpreted them, they didn't seem to me to be competent orders. On the contrary, they seemed idiotically unrealistic, poorly considered, and unwise. To have carried them out would have been a blunder bigger than letting the Hukk sneak in to Luna in the first place."

"Indeed, Admiral? And just what was your interpretation of the intent of those orders?"

"They didn't require much interpretation. They

were worded plainly enough; the idea was to kill off every last representative of the Hukk species—"

"Isn't that something of an exaggeration, Dalton? Your instructions were to cooperate with Admiral Borgman in eliminating the Hukk capability to wage war."

"Including wiping out their home world and all their colonies and outstations."

"Excuse me, Admiral Dalton." The reporter who had been anxiously hovering nearby spoke up. "Ah, sir, I wonder if you'd care to comment on a statement made earlier today by Senator Kelvin?" He drew a sheet of newsprint from a folder under his arm.

"I'd have to see it first," Dalton said casually.

The newsman offered the sheet, which was a galley proof of a pictonews page with a blurry photo of Dalton, Arianne and Senator Kelvin standing on a lawn before a colonnaded house. The headline read:

Man of the Hour Rapped by Sponsor

"In an exclusive interview with Worldpic columnist Mort Dunkel early today, Senator Rutherford Kelvin, the influential Hardliner chairman of the Senate Alien Relations Committee, stated that while he admired Rear Admiral Tancredi Dalton's handling of the Hukk force under First Admiral Saanch'k, it was unfortunate that prior to his self-detachment from the fleet under Admiral Starbird, Dalton had apparently misused certain confidential information with which the senator had entrusted the admiral."

"The fact of the matter," Dalton said, handing the page back to the newsman, "is that I didn't misuse any information given to me by Senator Kelvin; in fact, I made no use of it at all. I think that's what annoys him."

"I see, sir," the reporter said, looking hungrily at Dalton. "Now, if you could just tell me the nature of this confidential information—"

"Then it wouldn't be confidential, would it?" Dalton said.

The reporter's expression turned solemn. "There's another matter, Admiral, on which I feel sure you will wish to comment. Earlier today I was fortunate enough to have an opportunity to interview the Secretary of Defense at Bethesda. The Secretary categorically denied that he had issued any Special Order placing you in supreme command of the fleet and authorizing you to relieve Admiral Starbird."

Dalton nodded. "I see," he said. "Anything else?"

"I should think that would be quite sufficient, Admiral," the reporter said rather sharply.

"Sufficient for what, Mr. Dunkel?" Dalton asked, smiling slightly.

"Sufficient to completely discredit your statement before the committee to the effect that you were acting under departmental orders when you disregarded the orders of Admiral French relayed to you by Admiral Borgman—and, incidentally, sufficient to put an end to your Naval career."

"There's no conflict between my statement and what you say the Secretary said. I told the committee, quite accurately, that I acted under a Departmental Special Order."

"Isn't that a bit curious, Admiral? That the Secretary of Defense would be unaware that he had issued a highly controversial Special Order?"

"Let's not play word games," Dalton said. "I didn't say the order was issued by the Secretary; I said it was issued by the Office of the Secretary of Defense. I'm sure you're well aware that for the past year the Secretary has been a very sick man. Obviously the Department has continued to function in his absence."

The reporter stepped back, his cocky expression modified into one of mild perplexity.

"So that's how it is, Dalton?" Admiral Veidt spoke up as soon as the man was out of easy earshot. "You've cosied up to that Softlining traitor, Treech, have you? What did he offer you?"

"A crack at your job, Admiral," Dalton said off-handedly.

"You're doing all right for yourself out of this, aren't you, Dalton?" Veidt said, and half turned away. "So far, anyway. But there are still holes in your story you could con a battlewagon through. You're going to find out before this is over that you can't thumb your nose at higher authority and get away without a scratch."

"You can hoke up the Fleet Action Report any way you like, Veidt," Dalton said harshly at the other man's retreating back. "But when the committee sub-poenas my log tapes, there're going to be some red faces clashing with the Navy blue."

"Think again, Dalton," Veidt snapped, turning to stare angrily at him. "We had an idea you might put that bunch of political fuddy-duddies up to poking their noses into officially restricted Naval documents —but as it happens your log tapes don't seem to be available—if they ever existed."

"They exist, all right. Why shouldn't they? It's SOP to record all incoming and outgoing traffic as well as all command conversation on the bridge. It's all there, including French's damn fool Kill order. I suppose you and Borgman put him up to that piece of idiocy. French has always been a little xenophobic, but he's never come out in the open before as a copper-bottomed Hardliner."

"I've had enough of your damned impertinence, you young upstart." Veidt snarled and turned on his heel and collided with a flustered-looking aide, who scrambled hastily out of the great man's path.

The reporter bobbed up again at Dalton's elbow, looking eager. "If you have just one more moment, Admiral," he said in an ingratiating tone. "You said earlier that the terms of the Hukk treaty must embody certain realities in Hukk-Human relations. Now, since you've gone on record as having been the savior of the Hukk by refusing at the risk of your career to carry out an order to annihilate their fleet after it had surrendered to you, I assume that in spite of the rather truculent sound of your statement about the realities of Hukk-Human relations, that you favor passage of the treaty in its present form, which, as I'm sure you know, has been characterized as mush-headedly lenient by the Hardline party."

"I haven't seen the draft treaty," Dalton said. "However, I understand that it provides for the return to the Hukk of all armaments and weapons systems seized from them by us, including those removed from the vessels captured off Luna last month, as well as retention by the Hukk of all their outlying installations, scientific and openly military. And that it further provides for continued military aid as well as monetary grants. If there is any consideration granted in return to Terra, I am unaware of it. I'm completely opposed to any such treaty. The ability of the Hukk to wage war should be completely eliminated, and we'd be fools to give them any money or know-how that could be used against us. On the contrary, Leadpipe and Petreac should be ceded to us, and we should establish and maintain a permanent military enclave on the Hukk homeworld to keep an eye on them."

The reporter almost staggered back, looking dumfounded. "May I quote you on that, sir?" he said dubiously.

"Please do," Dalton said, and turned to see Admiral Veidt standing at his elbow.

"So you're changing your tack again, Dalton," the older man said, with an expression of distaste. "When you first sided with the Softliners I was surprised, because I never thought you were that kind of pantywaist. But frankly, I'd have had more respect for you if you'd stuck with your new friends, once you'd cast your lot with them. You're a bigger fool than I thought. You've played this whole thing as smooth as an acre of blast-burned concrete. By chickening out on your orders to destroy the Hukk war capability while we had them under our guns, you've alienated the Realists, or Hardliners, as the yellow press prefers to call us. Now, by giving that damned reporter a statement undercutting Treech's pet treaty, you'll have the Softliners down on you like a plague. I always thought that, whatever your shortcomings disciplinewise, you had some idea what you were doing, and were just getting your jollies by steering a perilous course through the political shoals. Now it appears you're just another blabbermouthed fool, cutting your throat every time you open your mouth. Well, bad cess to you, Dalton, in your new career, whatever it may be. I think you know you're washed up with the Navy."

"Thank you for your interest, Admiral," Dalton said, and saluted the senior officer crisply. Veidt replied with a sour look and a casual wave of his hand.

The eddying crowd separated the two admirals, and the bevy of newsmen scurried away, fanning out in all directions.

2

"When you set out to do a thing, you believe in doing it thoroughly, don't you, Tan?" Arianne said in a tone of barely restrained exasperation. "You had a perfect opportunity to become Ketchum's fair-haired boy. When word leaked to the press that you had intercepted a Hukk sneak force practically in our backyard, the public immediately began seeing you as the new George Washington, the savior of the people. Naturally, the Softliners didn't like it a bit: they felt that their protégés, the Hukk, had let them down badly by being caught with their hands in the cookie jar, and they took their resentment out on you. But when you went before the committee, all you had to do was make a few cooing noises, and you'd have had tough old Senator Ketchum and his whole Softliner party eating out of your hand. Instead of that, you got out your soapbox and made a speech about how the Hukk are a dangerous enemy.

"Fine, so you lose Ketchum and the Softliners, but you should have seen Daddy grin when he heard what you were saying. Right then, you could have mended your fences with Borgman and Veidt and all the other Hardlining Navy brass. That reporter, Mort whatsisname, would've given a beautiful play to the story if you'd explained that you'd been misunderstood and that you were all in favor of Ketchum's soft treaty. But instead of grabbing the opportunity, you wrecked yourself permanently with Veidt and Borgman and the High Command by practically dictating a draft for a Hardline treaty. Now, you don't have a friend left in either camp. Undersecretary Treech called Daddy this morning. He was furious. He accused Daddy of everything up to and including bribing you, with me as the bribe, believe it or not."

"That's too bad about Treech and Daddy," Dalton said unconcernedly. "I wasn't talking for their benefit."

"Whose benefit were you talking for? Certainly not your own."

"I don't want to sound like a comedian at such a solemn moment," Dalton said. "But I was talking for the benefit of the human race, of which I'm still proud to be a member, in spite of a lot of things. I don't want to see it eliminated in the struggle for survival of the fittest, just because we can't believe somebody a little smarter and tougher than we are is trying to eat us alive."

"Well, surely, Tan, now that the Hukk's grand strategy's failed, there's nothing more to worry about from that quarter."

"They'll probably play them close to their thoraces for a while," Dalton said. "But I wouldn't count on a permanent change in character, just because they'd had a little slap on the wrist."

"But the treaty, Tan—if the committee takes your ideas to heart and reports out a tough treaty, certainly that'll put an end to the problem once and for all."

"The tough treaty, as you put it, will only be as effective as its enforcement; and if we let the idea take root that the Hukk are just a bunch of misunderstood idealists, there'll be an outcry every time a clause of the treaty is invoked."

"So," Arianne said, "what are you going to do about it now? You've already thrown away your opportunity for a great Naval career. Surely you're not going to utterly destroy yourself by lobbying for what the media are calling the 'Dalton Plan.' "

"No, no lobbying," Dalton said. "What I do next isn't really up to me. I'm still under Navy orders, you know, until one o'clock this afternoon, at least. I understand Undersecretary Treech wants me on his carpet then."

"Well, placate him, Tan. You don't need to ruffle the poor old thing's feathers any further. Just be nice and nod and say 'yes' a few times. It might not hurt as much as you think it will."

"I'll give it a try," Dalton said. "I'll see you at dinner."

3

"I don't suppose that this will come as any surprise to you, Dalton," Deputy Secretary Treech said with as grim an expression as his flabby features would allow, "but you obviously have no future in this department. Accordingly you may consider yourself at liberty to accept an offer from private industry or to make whatever other plans you choose for whiling away the years between now and your funeral. By the way," he went on, "I'd be interested in knowing just what you have in mind. Out of a purely personal interest in your welfare, of course."

"Let me give the matter eight or ten seconds of deep thought," Dalton said. "Maybe I'll come up with something."

4

"But, Daddy! A junkyard!" Arianne wailed. She and her father were seated at either side of Dalton at the long table in the dining room of the Kelvin mansion at Arlington.

"Now, my girl, don't begin stigmatizing things with emotional labels," the senator reproved his daughter. "This is actually a magnificent opportunity for Tan, with half the Navy being scrapped out. His getting in on the ground floor in the bidding for salvage rights is worth a fortune. It was no routine task arranging for him to obtain those rights, I assure you."

"Oh, Daddy, I know you're trying to help, but it seems so degrading."

"Nonsense," the senator snapped. "He isn't going to be a rag and bone man, cruising back alleys and municipal dumps. His bid of a million and a half, which was accepted this afternoon by the Chief Disposal Agent of the Navy, is a very respectable one. He might have gotten the contract even without the word I dropped in the CDA's ear." The senator glanced up at Dalton. "How do *you* feel about it, Tan?" he inquired, with a lift of his eyebrows.

Dalton speared a prawn from the seafood cocktail before him. "Oh, it's what I always wanted, Senator, my very own salvage yard, where I can while away the long happy hours of my sunset years scrambling through the hulks of what used to be the Navy's fighting ships, prying an instrument face out of a panel here, rummaging through an overlooked footlocker there, playing back the logs and reminiscing about the old days and helping out distressed spacefarers with the odd nut and bolt and navigation set, all at a tidy profit."

Kelvin grimaced and removed a chip of crab shell from his mouth, glancing from Dalton to Arianne and back. "It's a perfectly respectable enterprise for a retired Navy man," he said. "Your acquisition of the franchise to operate on Grassroots was no small plum in itself. There's no doubt you'll turn a handsome profit with a location convenient to all of the major trade routes between Human and Hukk space. You'll be the sole on-the-scene source of supply of hard-to-get astrogational supplies. In a few years you'll be a wealthy man."

"But, Daddy!" Arianne cried. "Tan is a rear admiral. He's not a junk man. It's degrading."

"It will be good honest work," Dalton said. "As honest as anything can be that's launched in a flurry of string pulling. Not that I don't appreciate it, Senator," he said, glancing at the older man. "It would have been easy enough for you to just let me slide down the drain with the rest of the Navy in Treech's house-cleaning."

"It's not quite as bad as that, Dalton," Kelvin said. "The Fleet Space Arm is still in existence, with plenty of hardware and thousands of dedicated personnel. Treech didn't succeed in stripping us entirely naked."

"Thanks to Daddy and his friends," Arianne said.

"I'm still not crazy about Borgman and Veidt," Dalton said, "but I must admit they spoke up effectively against scrapping out every first-line ship we own."

"I've never felt any emotional kinship with the hard-core Hardlining military types," Kelvin said. "But you're right. Without their influence, I think Treech and his toadies would have succeeded in completely destroying our ability to defend ourselves."

"Tan, when can I come out and pay you a visit at Grassroots?" Arianne said.

"I suppose it will take me a few months to get things pulled into shape," Dalton said. "I'll let you know just as soon as I have a decent place in which to entertain a lady."

"Don't wait until you have a plush penthouse apartment completely equipped with wall-to-wall mood music," Arianne said, somewhat petulantly. "I don't mind roughing it a bit."

CHAPTER NINE

It was three months later, and Dalton, clad in faded khaki shirt and pants, was walking along the plank sidewalk that ran before the unpainted shops and offices lining the wide, dusty main street of Grassport, the largest settlement on the frontier planet Grassroots. He stopped before a building with a blue anodized aluminum facade above which the blue and white flag of United Terra hung limp in the still, hot air. A polished plate beside the large glass door bore the words GOVERNMENT HOUSE. Dalton pushed through the door into the cool hush of a wide lobby. He ignored the flutterings of a functionary in a badly cut suit of the style popular on Terra six months earlier.

"But really, sir!" the man called after him as he entered the lift. Dalton stepped off at the third floor and walked along the carpeted corridor to an immense door of polished mahogany on which was lettered in gold script:

OFFICE OF THE PLANETARY GOVERNOR
NO ADMITTANCE

Without pausing longer than was necessary to turn the brightly polished brass knob, Dalton stepped through the door and walked across the room. Under the window a man sat behind a wide, not-recently-polished desk. Dalton glanced at the scorched plastic-encased diagram he was holding in his hand and tossed it on the desk. The man seated there prodded the document with a stylus as if to see if there was any life left in it. He was a plump little man with a wide, brown, soft-leather face finely subdivided by a maze of hairlike wrinkles.

"Well, what's this supposed to be?" He had a brisk, no-nonsense voice, a voice that said it had places to go and things to do. He pushed out his lips and blinked up at the tall man leaning on his desk. Dalton swung a chair around and sat down.

"I closed up shop early today, Governor," he said, "and took a little run out past Dropoff and the Washboard. Just taking the air, not headed anywhere. About fifty miles west I picked up a radac pulse, a high one, coming in fast from off-planet."

Governor Marston frowned. "There's been no off-world traffic cleared into the port since the Three-Planet shuttle last Wednesday, Dalton. You must have been mistaken. You—"

"This one didn't bother with a clearance. He was headed for the desert, well away from any of the settlements."

"How do you know?"

"I tracked him. He saw me and tried some evasive

maneuvers, too close to the ground. He hit pretty hard."

"Good God, man! How many people were aboard? Were they killed?"

"No people were killed, Governor."

"I understood you to say—"

"Just the pilot," Dalton went on. "It was a Hukk scout boat."

Several expressions hovered over Governor Marston's mobile face; he chose amused disbelief.

"I see: you've been drinking. Or possibly this is your idea of hearty frontier humor."

"I took that off him." Dalton nodded at the plastic-covered paper on which a looping pattern of pale-blue lines was drawn. "It's a chart of the island. Being amphibious, the Hukk don't place quite the same importance on the interface between land and water that we do; they trace the contour lines right down past the shoreline, map sea bottoms and all. Still, you can pick out the outline easily enough."

"So?"

"The spot marked with the pink circle was what he was interested in. He crumped in about ten miles short of it."

"What the devil would a Hukk scout boat be looking for out there?" the governor said in a voice from which all the snap had drained.

"He was making a last-minute confirmation check on a landing site."

"A landing site—for what?"

"Maybe I should have said beachhead?"

"What kind of nonsense is this, Dalton? A beachhead?"

"Nothing elaborate. Just a small commando-type operation, about a hundred troops, light armor, hand weapons, limited objectives—"

"Dalton, what is this?" the official exploded. "It's been only seven months since we beat the Hukk into the ground! They know better than to start anything now!"

2

Dalton turned the chart over and pushed it toward the governor. There were complex characters scrawled in columns across it.

"What am I supposed to make of this . . . this Chinese laundry list?" the governor snapped.

"It's a brief of a Hukk Order of Battle. Handwritten notes probably jotted down by the pilot, against regulations."

"Are you seriously suggesting the Hukk are planning an invasion?"

"The advance party is due in about nine hours," Dalton said. "The main force—about five thousand troops, heavy equipment—is standing by off-planet, waiting to see how it goes."

"This is fantastic! Invasions don't happen like this! Just . . . just out of a clear sky!"

"You expect them to wait for a formal invitation?"

"How do you know all this?"

"It's all there. The scout was a fairly high-ranking intelligence officer. He may even have planned the operation."

The governor gave an indignant grunt, then pursed his lips, pushing his brows together. "See here, if this fellow you intercepted doesn't report back—"

"His report went out right on schedule."

"You said he was killed!"

"I used his comm gear to send the prearranged signal. Just a minimike pulse on the Hukk LOS freke."

"You warned them off?"

Dalton shook his head. "I gave them the all clear. They're on the way here now, full gate and warheads primed."

The governor grabbed up his stylus and threw it at the desk. It bounced across the floor.

"Get out of here, Dalton! You've had your fun! I could have you thrown into prison for this! If you imagine I have nothing better to do than listen to the psychotic imaginings of a broken-down social misfit—"

"If you'd like to send someone out to check," Dalton cut in, "they'll find the Hukk scout boat right where I left it."

Governor Marston sat with his mouth open, eyes glued to Dalton.

"You're out of your mind. Even if you did find a wrecked boat—and I'm not conceding you did—how would you know how to make sense of their pothooks?"

"I learned quite a bit about the Hukk at the Command and Staff school."

"At the Com—" The governor barked a laugh. "Oh, certainly, the Admiralty opens up the Utter Top Secret C&S school to tourists on alternate Thursdays. You took two weeks off from your junk business to drop over and absorb what it takes a trained expert two years to learn."

"Three years," Dalton said. "And that was before I was in the junk business."

The governor looked Dalton up and down with sudden uncertainty. "Are you hinting that you're a . . . a retired commodore, or something of the sort?"

"Not exactly a commodore," Dalton said. "And not exactly retired."

"Eh?"

"I was invited to resign—during the Hukk treaty debates."

The governor looked blank, then startled.

"You're not . . . *that* Dalton?"

"If I am—you'll concede I might know the Hukk handscript?"

3

The governor rammed himself bolt upright.

"Why, I have a good mind to—" he broke off. "Dalton, as soon as word gets around who you are, you're finished here! There's not a man on Grassroots who'd do business with a convicted traitor!"

"The charge was insubordination, Governor."

"I remember the scandal well enough. You fought the treaty, went around making speeches undermining public confidence in the Admiralty that had just saved their necks from a Hukk take-over! Oh, I remember you, all right! Hardline Dalton! Going to grind the beaten foe down under a booted heel! One of those ex-soldiers-turned-rabble-rouser!"

"Which leaves us with the matter of a Hukk force nine hours out of Grassroots."

"Bah, I . . ." The governor paused, twisting in his chair. "Man, are you sure of this?" He muttered the words from the corner of his mouth, as if trying to avoid hearing them.

Dalton nodded.

"All right," the governor said, reaching for the screen. "Subject to a check, of course, I'll accept your story. I'll notify CDT HQ at Croanie. If this is what you say it is, it's a gross breach of the treaty—"

"What can Croanie do? The official Love Thine Enemy line ties their hands. A public acknowledgment of a treaty violation by the Hukk would discredit the whole Softline party—including some of the top Admiralty brass and half the major candidates in the upcoming elections. They won't move—even if they had anything to move with, and if they could get it here in time."

"What are you getting at?"

"It's up to *us* to stop them, Governor."

"Us—stop an armed force of trained soldiers? That's Admiralty business, Dalton!"

"Maybe—but it's *our* planet. We have guns and men who know how to use them."

"There are other methods than armed force for handling such matters, Dalton! A few words in the right quarter—"

"The Hukk deal in actions. Seven months ago they tried and missed. Now they're moving a new pawn out onto the board. That makes it our move."

"Well—suppose they do land a small party in the desert. Perhaps they're carrying out some sort of scientific mission, perhaps they don't even realize the world is occupied. After all, there are less than half a million colonists here . . ."

Dalton was smiling a little. "Do you believe that, Governor?"

"No, damn it! But it *could* be that way!"

"You're playing with words, Marston. The Hukk aren't wasting time talking."

"And your idea is . . . is to confront them—"

"Confront, hell," Dalton growled. "I want a hundred militiamen who know how to handle a gun; the blast rifles locked up in the local armory will do. We'll pick our spots and be waiting for them when they land."

"You mean—ambush them?"

"You could call it that," Dalton said indifferently.

"Well . . ." The governor looked grave. "I could point out to the Council that in view of the nature of this provocative and illegal act on the part of—"

"Sure," Dalton cut off the speech. "I'll supply transport from my yard; there's an old ore tug that will do the job. You can make it legal later. Right now I need an authorization to inspect the armory."

"Well . . ." Frowning, the governor spoke a few words into the dictyper, snatched the slip of paper as it popped from the slot, signed it with a slash of the stylus.

"Have the men alerted to report to the arms depot at twenty-two hundred hours," Dalton said as he tucked the chit away. "In field uniform, ready to move out."

"Don't start getting too big for your breeches yet, Dalton!" the governor barked. "None of this is official; you're still just the local junkman as far as I'm concerned."

"While you're at it, you'd better sign a commission for me as a lieutenant of militia, Governor. We may have a guardhouse lawyer in the bunch."

"Rather a comedown for a former rear admiral, isn't it?" Marston said with a slight lift of the lip. "I think we'll skip that. You'd better just sit tight until the Council acts."

"Twenty-two hundred, Governor," Dalton said. "That's cutting it fine. And tell them to eat a good dinner. It may be a long wait for breakfast."

4

The Federation Post Office was a blank gray five-story front of local granite, the biggest and ugliest building in the territorial capital. Dalton went in along a well-lit corridor lined with half-glass doors, went through the one lettered TERRAN SPACE ARM, and below, in smaller letters, *Sgt. Brunt—Recruiting Officer.* Behind the immaculate counter decorated with colorful posters of clear-eyed young models in smart uniforms, a thick-necked man of medium height and age, with a tanned face and close-cropped sandy hair, looked up from the bare desk with an expression of cheerful determination that underwent an invisible change to wary alertness as his eyes flicked over his caller.

"Good morning, Sergeant," Dalton said. "I understand you hold the keys to the weapons storage shack north of town."

Brunt thought that over, nodded once. His khakis were starched and creased to a knife-edge. A combat crew badge glinted red and gold over his left shirt pocket.

Dalton handed over the slip of paper the governor had signed. Brunt read it, frowned faintly, read it again, folded it, and tapped it on the desk.

"What's it all about, Dalton?" He had a rough-edged voice.

"For now that has to be between the governor and me, Brunt."

Brunt snapped a finger at the note. "I'd like to oblige the governor," he said, "but the weapons storage facility is a security area. No civilians allowed in, Dalton." He tossed the note across the desk.

Dalton nodded. "I should have thought of that," he said. "Excuse the interruption."

"Just a minute," Brunt said sharply as Dalton turned away. "If you'd like to tell me what's behind this—"

"Then you might stretch a regulation, eh? No thanks, Sergeant. I couldn't ask you to do that."

As Dalton left, Brunt was reaching for his desk screen.

5

Dalton lived a mile from town in a small prefab at the side of a twenty-acre tract covered with surplus military equipment, used mining rigs, salvaged transport units, from crawlers to pogos. He parked his car behind the house and walked back between the looming hulks of gutted lighters, stripped shuttle craft ten years obsolete, wrecked private haulers, to a big use-scarred cargo carrier. He started it up, maneuvered it around to the service ramp at the back, spent ten minutes checking it over. In the house, he ate a hasty meal, packed more food in a carton, changed clothes. He strapped on a well-worn service pistol, pulled on a deck jacket. He cranked up the cargo hauler, steered it out to the highway. It was a ten-minute drive past the two-factory heavy-industry belt, past scattered truck gardens, on another three miles into the pink-chalk, ravine-sliced countryside. The weapons depot was a ribbed-metal Quonset perched on a rise of ground to the left of the road. Dalton turned off, pulled to a stop, and waited for the dust to settle before stepping down from the high cab.

There was a heavy combination lock on the front door. It took Dalton ten minutes with a heavy-duty cutter to open it. Inside the long, narrow building, he switched on an unshielded overhead light. There was a patina of dust over the weapons racked in lock frames along the walls.

Aother three minutes with the cutter had the lock bars off the racks. The weapons were 2-mm Norges, wartime issue, in fair shape. The charge indicators registered nil.

There was a charging unit against the end wall, minus the energy coil. Dalton went out to the big vehicle, opened the access hatch, lifted out the heavy power unit, lugged it inside, used cables to jump it to the charger.

It took him an hour and thirty-eight minutes to put a full charge on each of one hundred and two weapons. It was twenty-one thirty when he put through a call on the vehicle's talker to the office of the governor. The answering circuit informed him that the office was closed. He tried the gubernatorial residence and was advised that the governor was away on official business. As he switched off, a small blue-painted copter with an Admiralty eagle and the letters FSA on the side settled in beside him. The hatch popped open and Sergeant Brunt emerged. crisp in his khakis. He stood, fists on hips, looking up at the hauler's cab.

"All right, Dalton," he called. "Game's over. You can haul that clanker back to the yard. Nobody's coming—and you're not going anywhere."

"I take it that's a message from his Excellency the Governor?" Dalton said.

Brunt's eyes strayed past the big vehicle to the shed door, marred by a gaping hole where the lock had been.

"What the—?" Brunt's hand went to his hip, came up gripping a palm gun.

"Drop it," Dalton said.

Brunt froze. "Dalton, you're already in plenty of trouble—"

"The gun, Brunt."

Brunt tossed the small gun to the ground. Dalton climbed down, his pistol in his hand.

"The Council said no, eh?"

"What did you expect, you fool? You want to start a war?"

"No—I want to finish one." Dalton jerked his head. "Inside."

Brunt preceded him into the hut and, at Dalton's direction, gathered up half a dozen recharged weapons, touching only the short, thick barrels. He carried them out and stowed them in the rear of the hauler.

Dalton ordered Brunt into the cab, climbed up beside him. As he did, Brunt aimed a punch at his head; Dalton blocked it and caught his wrist.

"I've got thirty pounds and the reach on you, Sergeant," he said. "Just sit quietly. Under the circumstances I'm glad you happened along." He punched the door-lock key, started up, lifted onto the air cushion and headed west into the desert.

6

Dusk was trailing purple veils across the sky when Dalton pulled the carrier in under a wind-carved wing of violet chalk at the base of a jagged rock wall and cut power. Brunt grumbled but complied when Dalton ordered him out of his seat.

"We've got a little scramble ahead, Sergeant."
Dalton glanced up the craggy slope looming above.

"You could have picked an easier way to go off your
rails," the recruiter said. "Suppose I won't go?"

Dalton smiled faintly, doubled his right fist, and ro-
tated it against his left palm. Brunt spat.

"If I hadn't been two years in a lousy desk job, I'd
take you, Dalton, reach or no reach."

"Just pick up the guns, Brunt."

After a stiff climb, it took Dalton most of an hour to
place the five extra blast rifles in widely spaced positions around the crater's half-mile rim, propping
them firmly, aimed at the center of the rock-strewn
natural arena below. Brunt laughed at him.

"The old Fort Zinderneuf game, eh? But you don't
have any corpses to man the ramparts."

"Over there, Brunt—where I can keep an eye on
you." Dalton settled himself behind a shielding growth
of salt weed, sighting along the barrel of the blast rifle.
Brunt watched with a sour smile.

"You really hate these fellows, don't you, Dalton?
You were out to get them with the treaty, and failed,
and now you've going to even it all up, single-handed."

"Not quite single-handed. There are two of us."

"You can kidnap me at gun point, Dalton, and you
can bring me out here. But you can't make me fight."

"That's right."

Brunt made a disgusted sound. "You crazy fool!
You'll get us both killed!"

"I'm glad you concede the possibility that this isn't
just a party of picnickers we're here to meet."

"What do you expect, if you open fire on them?"

"I expect them to shoot back."

"Can you blame them?" Brunt retorted.

Dalton shook his head. "But that doesn't mean I
have to let them get away with it."

"You know, Dalton, at the time of your court, I wondered about a few things. Maybe I even had a few doubts about the treaty myself. But this"—he waved a hand that took in the black desert, the luminous horizon, the sky—"confirms everything they threw at you. You're a paranoiac—"

"But I can still read Hukk cursive," Dalton said. He pointed overhead. A flickering point of pink light was barely visible against the violet sky.

"I think you know a Hukk drive when you see one," Dalton said. "Now let's watch and see whether it's stuffed eggs or blast cannon they brought along."

7

"It doesn't make sense," Brunt growled. "We've shown them we can whip them in war; we gave them generous peace terms, let them keep their space capability almost intact, even offered them economic aid—"

"While we scrapped the fighting ships that we didn't build until ten years of Hukk raids forced us to."

"I know the Hardline, Dalton. OK, you told 'em so. Maybe there was something in it. But what good is this caper supposed to do? You want to be a martyr, is that it? And I'm the witness—"

"Not quite. I think the Hukk picked this spot because it's well shielded from casual observation, close enough to Grassport and Bedrock to launch a quick strike, but not so close as to be stumbled over. That's sound, as far as it goes, but as a defensive position, it couldn't be worse. Of course, they didn't expect to have to defend it."

"Look, Dalton, OK, you were right, the Hukk are

making an unauthorized landing on Grassroots' soil. Maybe they're even an armed party, as you said. Swell. I came out here with you, I've seen the ship, and I'll testify. So why louse it up? We'll pass the file to the CDT and let them handle it! It's their baby, not yours! Not mine! We've got no call to get ourselves blasted to kingdom come playing One Man Task Force!"

"You think Croanie will move in fast and slap 'em down?"

"Well . . . it might take some time—"

"Meanwhile the Hukk will have brought in their heavy stuff. They'll entrench half a mile under the surface and then start spreading out. By the time the Navy gets into the act, they'll hold half the planet."

"All right! Is that fatal? We'll negotiate, arrange for the release of Terry nationals, the return of Terry property—"

"Compromise, in other words."

"All right, you give a little, you get a little!"

"And the next time?"

"What next time?"

"The Hukk will take half of Grassroots with no more expense than a little time at a conference table. That will look pretty good to them. A lot better than an all-fronts war. Why gulp, when you can nibble?"

"If they keep pushing, we'd slap them down. You know that."

"Sure we will—in time. Why not do it now?"

"Don't talk like a fool, Dalton! What can one man do?"

The Hukk ship was visibly lower now, drifting down silently on the stuttering column of light that was its lift beam. It was dull black, bottle-shaped, with a long ogee curve to the truncated prow.

"If I had any heavy stuff up here, I'd go for her

landing jacks," Dalton said. "But a 2-mm Norge doesn't pack enough wallop to be sure of crippling her. And if I miss her, they're warned: they can lift and cook us with an ion bath. So we'll wait until they're off-loaded, then pour it into the port. That's a weak spot on a Hukk ship. The iris is fragile, and any malfunction there means no seal, ergo no lift. Then we settle down to picking them off, officers first. With fast footwork, we should have them trimmed down to manageable size before they can organize a counterattack."

"What if I don't go along with this harebrained suicide scheme?"

"Then I'll have to wire your wrists and ankles."

"And if you're killed, where does that leave me?"

"Better make up your mind."

"Suppose I shoot at you instead of them?"

"In that case I'd have to kill you."

"You're pretty sure of yourself, Dalton." When Dalton didn't answer, Brunt licked his lips and said: "I'll go this far: I'll help you burn the port, because if you foul it up it's my neck, too. But as for shooting fish in a barrel—negative, Dalton."

"I'll settle for that."

"But afterwards, once she's grounded—all bets are off."

"Tell that to the Hukk," Dalton said.

8

"Lousy light for this work," Brunt said over his gunsights. Dalton, watching the Hukk ship settle almost soundlessly in a roil of dust, didn't answer. Suddenly, floodlights flared around the base of the ship, bathing it in a reflected violet glow as, with a grating of metal against rock, the Hukk vessel came to rest.

"Looks like a stage all set up for *Swan Lake*," Brunt muttered.

For five minutes, nothing happened. Then the circular exit valve dilated, spilling a widening shaft of green light out in a long path across the crater floor, casting black shadows behind the thickly scattered boulders. A silhouette moved in the aperture, jumped down, a long-legged shadow matching its movements as it stepped aside. Another followed, and more, until five Hukk stood outside the ship. They were slope-backed quadrupeds, hunched, neckless, long-faced, knob-jointed, pendulous-bellied, leathery-hided. A cluster of sheathed digital numbers lay on either side of the slablike cheeks.

"Ugly bastids," Brunt said. "But that's got nothing to do with it, of course."

Now more troops were emerging, falling-in in orderly rows. At a command faintly audible to Dalton as a squeaky bark, a squad of ten Hukk about-faced and marched fifty feet from the ship, halted, opened ranks.

"Real parade-ground types," Brunt said. "Kit inspection, no less."

"What's the matter, Sergeant? Annoyed they didn't hit the beach with all guns blazing?"

"Dalton, it's not too late to change your mind."

"I'm afraid it is—by about six and a half years."

The disembarkation proceeded with promptness and dispatch. It was less than ten minutes before nine groups of ten Hukk had formed up, each with an officer in charge. At a sharp command, they wheeled smartly, executed a complicated maneuver which produced a single hollow square two Hukk deep around the baggage stacked at the center.

"All right, Brunt, off-loading complete," Dalton said. "Commence firing on the port."

The deep *chuff! chuff!* of the blast rifles echoed back

from the far side of the crater as the two guns opened up. Brilliant flashes winked against the ship. The Hukk stood fast, with the exception of two of the officers, who whirled and ran for the ship. Dalton switched sights momentarily, dropped the first one, then the second, returned to the primary target.

Now the square broke suddenly, but not in random fashion; each side peeled away as a unit, spread out, hit the dirt, each Hukk scrambling for shelter, while the seven remaining officers took up their positions in the centers of their respective companies. In seconds the dispersed troops were virtually invisible. Here and there the blink and *pop!* of return fire crackled from behind a boulder or a gully.

The ship's port was glowing cherry red; the iris seemed to be jammed, half-closed. Dalton shifted targets, settled the cross-hairs on an officer, fired, switched to another as the first fell. He killed three before the remaining Hukk brasshat scuttled for the protection of a ridge of rock. Without a pause Dalton turned his fire on the soldiers scattered across the open ground.

"Stop, you bloodthirsty fool!" Brunt was yelling. "The ship's crippled, the officers are dead! The poor devils are helpless down there—"

There was a violet flash from near the ship, a deep-toned *war-hoom!*, a crashing fall of rock twenty feet to their left. A second flash, a second report, more rock exploded, closer.

"Time to go," Dalton snapped and, without waiting to see Brunt's reaction, slid down the backslope, scrambled along it while rock chips burst from the ridge above him amid the smashing impacts of the Hukk power cannon. He surfaced two hundred yards to the left of his original position, found the rifle emplacement. He re-aimed the weapon, depressed the trigger and set the hold-down for automatic rapid fire, paused long enough to fire half a dozen aimed bolts at the enemy, then moved on to the next gun to repeat the operation, leaving the unmanned weapon firing toward the ship.

9

Twenty minutes later Dalton, halfway around the crater from his original location, paused for a breather, listening to the steady crackle of the Hukk return fire, badly aimed but intense enough to encourage him to keep his head down. As well as he could judge, he had so far accounted for eight Hukk troopers in addition to several officers. Of the five blast rifles he had left firing on automatic, two had been knocked out or had exhausted their charges. The other three were still firing steadily, kicking pits in the bare rock below.

A few of the ship's ground lights were still on; the rest had been shot out by the Hukk soldiery. By their glow Dalton picked an exposed target near the ship, brought his rifle to bear on him. He was about to pull the trigger when he saw Brunt sliding downslope thirty degrees around the perimeter of the ring wall from him, waving an improvised white flag.

10

The words from the Hukk PA system were loud and clear if somewhat echoic, and were delivered in excellent Terran, marred only by the characteristic Hukk difficulty with nasals:

"Terran hwarrior," the deep, booming voice rolled across the crater. "Hwe know hnow that you are alone. You have fought hwell. Hnow you must surrender or be destroyed."

The lone Hukk officer stood in an exposed position near the center of the semicircular dispersement of soldiers, holding the end of a rope which was attached to Brunt's neck.

"Unless you show yourself at once," the amplified voice boomed out, "you hwill be hunted out and killed."

The Hukk officer turned to Brunt. A moment later Brunt's hoarse voice echoed across the crater:

"For God's sake, Dalton, they're giving you a chance! Throw down your gun and surrender!"

Sweat trickled down across Dalton's face. He wiped it away, cupped his hands beside his mouth, and shouted in the Hukk language:

"Release the prisoner first."

There was a pause. "You offer an exchange, himself for yourself?"

"That's right."

Another pause. "Very well, I accept," the Hukk called. "Come forward now. I assure you safe-conduct."

Dalton lifted his pistol from its holster, tucked it inside his belt, under the jacket. He studied the ground below, then worked his way fifty feet to the right before he stood, the blast gun in his hands, and started down the slope along the route he had selected, amid a rattle of dislodged rock fragments.

"Throw down your weapon!" the PA ordered as he reached the crater floor. Dalton hesitated, then tossed the gun aside. Empty-handed, he advanced among the boulders toward the waiting Hukk. The captain— Dalton was close enough to see his rank badge now— had pulled Brunt in front of him. The latter, aware of his role as a human shield, looked pale and damp. His mouth twitched as though there were things it wanted to say, but was having trouble finding words equal to the occasion.

When Dalton was twenty feet from the Hukk officer, passing between two six-foot-high splinters of upended rock, he halted abruptly. At once, the captain barked an order. There was a flicker of motion to Dalton's left. He darted a hand under his jacket, came out with the pistol, fired, and was facing the officer again as a yapping wail came from the Hukk he had wounded.

"Tell your troops to throw down their guns and pull back," Dalton said crisply.

"You call on me to surrender?" The officer was carefully keeping his members in Brunt's shadow.

"You've been had, Captain. Only three of your soldiers can bear on me here—and they have to expose themselves to fire. My reaction time is quicker than theirs."

"You bluff—"

"The gun in my hand will penetrate two inches of flint steel," Dalton said. "The man in front of you is a lot softer than armor."

"You would kill the man for whose freedom you offered your life?"

"What do you think?"

"My troops surely will kill you!"

"Probably. But *you* won't be here to transmit the all-clear to the boys standing by off-planet."

"Then what do you hope to gain, man?"

"Dalton's the name, Captain."

"That name is known to me. I am Ch'oova. I was with the Grand Armada at Luna."

"The Grand Armada planned well—but not quite well enough."

"True, Admiral. Perhaps our strategy has been at fault." The captain raised his head, barked an order.

Hukk soldiers began rising from concealment, gun muzzles pointing at the ground; they cantered away toward the ship by twos and threes, their small hooves raising cottony puffs of dust.

When they were alone, Captain Ch'oova tossed the rope aside.

"I think," he said, with a small, formal curtsy, "that we had best negotiate."

11

"That fellow Ch'oova told me something funny," Brunt said as the cargo carrier plowed toward the dawn. "Seven months ago, at Luna, you were in command of the fleet after Admiral Starbird was relieved. You were the one who brought the Grand Armada to a standstill."

"I took over from Starbird, yes."

"And captured the Hukk fleet. Funny, that part didn't get in the papers. But not so funny, maybe, at that. According to Ch'oova, after the fighting was over, you refused a direct Admiralty order."

"Garbled transmission," Dalton said.

"Tempers run high in wartime," Brunt said. "The Hukk had made a lot of enemies before we finally faced up to the facts. The High Command wanted a permanent solution. They gave you secret orders to accept the Hukk surrender and then blow them out of space. You said no."

"Not really; I just didn't get around to carrying out the Kill order."

"And in a few days, cooler heads prevailed. But not before you were relieved and moved to a desk job, and your part in the victory covered up."

"Just a routine transfer," Dalton said.

"And then, by God, you turned around . . . you, the white-haired boy who'd saved the brass from making a blunder that would have ruined them when it got known—you went after the treaty hammer and tongs, to toughen it up. First you save the Hukk's necks— and then you break yourself trying to tighten the screws on them."

Dalton shook his head. "Nope; I just didn't want to mislead them."

"You wanted their armada broken up, occupation of their principal worlds, arms limitations with inspections—"

"Brunt, this night's work cost the lives of fourteen Hukk soldiers, most of them probably ordinary citizens who were drafted and sent out here all full of patriotic fervor. That was a dirty trick. We beat them once. Then we picked 'em up, dusted 'em off, and gave them back their toys. That wasn't fair to a straightforward bunch of opportunists like the Hukk. It was an open invitation to blunder again. And unless they were slapped down quick, they'd keep on blundering in deeper—until they goaded us into building another fleet. And this time, there might not be enough pieces left to pick up."

Brunt sat staring thoughtfully out at the paling sky ahead; he laughed shortly. "When you went steaming out there with fire in your eye, I thought you were out for revenge on the Hukk for losing you your fat career. But you were just delivering a message."

"In terms that they could understand," Dalton said.

"You're a strange man, Admiral. For the second time, single-handed, you've stopped a war. And because you agreed with Ch'oova to keep the whole thing confidential, no one will ever know. Result: you'll be a laughingstock for your false alarm. And with your identity known, you're washed up in the junk business. Hell, Marston will have the police waiting to pick you up for everything from arms theft to spitting on the sidewalk. And you can't say a word in your own defense."

"It'll blow over."

"I could whisper a word in Marston's ear—"

"No, you won't, Brunt. And if you do, I'll call you a liar. I gave Ch'oova my word; if this caper became public knowledge, it would kick the Hukk out of every Terran market they've built up."

"Looks like you've boxed yourself into a corner, Admiral," Brunt said softly.

"That's twice you've called me admiral—Major."

Brunt made a surprised sound. Dalton gave him a one-sided smile.

"I can spot a hotshot Intelligence type at half a mile. I used to wonder why they posted you out here."

"To keep an eye on you, Admiral, what else?"

"Me?"

"A man like you is an enigma. You had the brass worried. You didn't hew to any party line. But I think you've gotten the message across now—and not just to the Hukk."

Dalton grunted.

"So I think I can assure that you won't need to look for a new place to start up your junkyard. I think the Navy needs you. It'll take some string pulling, but it can be done. Maybe not as an admiral—not for a while—but at least you'll have a deck under your feet. How does it sound?"

"I'll think about it," Dalton said.